An Expanse *of* Blue

An Expanse of Blue

KAUAKANILEHUA MĀHOE ADAMS

Heartdrum
An Imprint of HarperCollinsPublishers

HarperCollins Children's Books, a division of
HarperCollins Publishers, 195 Broadway, New York, NY 10007

HarperCollins Publishers, Macken House,
39/40 Mayor Street Upper, Dublin 1, D01 C9W8, Ireland

Heartdrum is an imprint of HarperCollins Publishers.

An Expanse of Blue

harpercollins.com

Library of Congress Control Number: 2026931987
ISBN 978-0-06-341795-3

Typography by Molly Fehr
26 27 28 29 30 LBC 5 4 3 2 1
First Edition

For all the Kānaka kids growing up in the diaspora
trying
to
find
the
path
back
home.
Look
to our
ancestors;
they
guide
the
way.

And for my Aunty Marie, who visited me in a dream
to let me know my papa was safe
on the other side.

Part One

Like cages full of birds, so are their houses full of deceit.

Jeremiah 5:27

January 25

Third Sunday in Ordinary Time

Mass begins at 10:00 a.m. on the dot,
but we are late
because I walked out of my room this morning
in leggings and a sweatshirt and
Dad
lost
his
shit.

Now he leads the charge across the packed parking lot,
checking over his shoulder to make sure we're all still there

while Mama grips my hand like I'm a little kid,
like she's worried I'm going to try to escape.

My sister struggles to keep up with us
in the ridiculous heels she insists on wearing,
and I can feel her rage rolling off her in waves,

because the only thing my sister can't stand more than me
is being tardy.
Caw!

A crow takes off from atop the statue of Saint Peter presiding
over the front steps.

My eyes track its path across the overcast sky until
it disappears between two proud standing oaks, and I envy

the way the crow was made
for soaring.

I was made for no such thing.

I was made
to make everyone
late.

It's 10:12 a.m.
Mass has already begun,
but we are late
because
good!
girls!
don't!
wear!
leggings!
to!
church!

And they
certainly
don't talk back
when they're
being
talked to.
We are late
because
I dared
to be
something
other
than a
good girl.
We
are
late
because
of

me.

Dad rushes us through the double doors
and into the cavernous church narthex.

Frigid

        air

pumping

            out

of a white machine
blasts me hard in the face

even though it's January in Hawk Valley, Washington,
and none of us have seen the sun
in weeks.

An elderly usher guards the entrance to the nave,
frowning at our late arrival.

He holds up a hand to stop us in our tracks.

    Dad huffs air out his nose,
    the tiniest fraction of his anger breaking the surface.
    Still   he manages to hold his tongue.

Through the glass-paned doors Father Ambrose
stands at the pulpit in bright green robes,
and his opening prayer is distorted by the wall between us,
making him sound like the voice of God

Himself.

I hate the smell of this place.
It reeks like someone used bleach to try to mask the stench
of incense and old bodies.

Tried and
failed.

I shove the sleeve of the "respectable" dress
Mama made me change into
against my nose and

I
don't
care

that the usher notices.

I don't care that his frown
has deepened so intensely that the corners of his mouth
might just touch—

"Cut it out," Dad snaps at me.

I drop my arm.

Bleach
body
and ash

assault my senses,

making my eyes water—
fantastic,
now everyone is going to think I'm crying.

I
really,
really
hate
                    the smell of
this place.

The usher jerks his chin toward the chapel
just
          as
the congregation
takes a seat
in unison.

Time to go inside.
Everyone is going to stare at us.

Dad nudges Kāia. "Don't drag your feet."
Her heels pick up—

click
          clack
                    click—

but I stay put.

"Be good." Mama yanks me to her side
and hauls me forward with her. "For me."

Mama tries her best.
But I am trying my best, too.

She squeezes my shoulder hard,
and it feels nothing like a hug

and everything like a cage.

At the entrance to the nave
stands a massive stone baptismal font
    that's big enough for Father Ambrose to wade in
    whenever there is a baby to be baptized.

As I dip my fingers into the cool water,
I wish I could slip all the way in
and
sink
right
down
to
the
bottom
to let it wash me clean
of this morning for good.

Mama pricks the surface of the water with her finger,
sending out ripples of perfect circles.

She is the picture of a godly woman,
with her eyes cast low as she signs the cross.
    "Don't forget your prayers, Aouli."

Dear God,
My name is Aouli Elizabeth Smith.

Aouli (*Hawaiian*) meaning
blue, sky, expanse.

> My soul is great,
> sweeping like the sky
> and a thousand different shades
> of blue.

Elizabeth (*Hebrew*) meaning
my God is an oath.

> My body is a promise
> I didn't make
> to a God I've never seen.

Smith (*German*) meaning
to strike, to smite.

> My heart is made
> of only sharp edges,
> fashioned to cut
> from the inside out.

Aouli Elizabeth Smith (*origin unknown*) meaning
a thing unintentionally made.

In the name of the
Father,
Daughter,
and the Holy Something—

Amen.

PS
But most people
can't say my name

so everyone (except my family)
just calls me

Lily.

Amen

again.

I'm glad we're late, even though

Kāia is embarrassed
and Mama is upset
and I can see Dad's anger
simmering
beneath
his skin
every
time
he
looks
at

me.

I am still glad
because the only place left
for us to sit

is in the back,

and the back is
the perfect place
for me

to watch Damien Miller
run his fingers through his yellow hair.

The perfect place
for me

to pretend that it's actually my hair
his fingers sweep through.

The perfect place
for me

to indulge in every thought I've ever had
about Damien's fingers and *me*.

The perfect place
for me

to hide the heat stirring
low in my belly.

The perfect place
for me

to let my fantasies sprout
wings and fly free

because there's no way
God can hear me

from all the way back here.

Texts

10:42 a.m.

Me: Why are you not at mass today?

Me: What the hell?!?!

Taylor: I'm at Gram's for the weekend rememberrrrr?

Me: Gram doesn't go to mass?

Taylor: No

Taylor: She makes us watch it on her tv

Me: EW

Taylor: Right?

Me: Well you suck

Taylor: Rude.

10:51 a.m.

Me: :(

Me: I wish you were here

Taylor: That's what I thought!!

Taylor Mackenzie has been my best friend
since our mothers met at Mommy and Me Bible Study
when we were toddlers—

and she's the only reason
church is ever

almost

sort of

semi

bearable,

which makes this crappy-ass morning
that much
ass-crappier.

Donuts are served every Sunday
in the church basement by the Cavaliers of Christ—

a parish club of middle-aged men
bound together by their dedication to the church
(and lack of other hobbies).

The donuts are supposed to be an after-mass treat
for those who keep to their holy fast.

Catholics aren't allowed to eat before church
for some dumb reason
that my parents never really explained to me.

They tend to do that.

A lot.

My family waits silently
in a long line for donuts that extends out of the basement
and back up the stairs to the narthex.

Parishioners' chatter resounds off the yellowing walls,
making the massive room feel small and inescapable

while the residual tension from Dad's blowup this morning
is so   thick

I can feel it
pushing us   farther and   farther apart—

"Aouli, watch where you're standing." Dad grabs my elbow,
jerking me toward him to allow an elderly couple to pass.

I mumble an apology at their backs,
                    but I don't think they hear me.

Kāia frowns. "You were standing in the middle of the walkway."

"You need to be more aware of your surroundings,"
Dad scolds me under his breath.

I glance at Mama for a way out,   a path for escape,
but she's busy
pretending
she can't see me.

When we reach the front of the line
Mr. Stevens is there with a smile and a napkin for each of us.

Mr. Stevens is Julie Stevens's dad.

Julie is a senior in our youth group
and Kāia's only friend at church.

Kāia's only friend, *period*.

Dad gives him a firm shake. "How are you, Joel?"

"Can't complain!" Mr. Stevens chuckles.

Mama quietly accepts a napkin for a donut she will pick at,
but never actually eat, just to be polite,

while Kāia dodges his offering
with Olympic-athlete-level agility.

"Hey there, Miss Lily." Mr. Stevens sweeps out his arm,
presenting the table of donuts packed neatly in pink boxes.
"Got a good batch just for you today."

They're the same donuts they always have,

but it is nice to pretend that these ones are special
just for me.

I pick out a donut with sprinkles
and bite into it immediately.

"Are you not going to eat a donut?"

I ask Kāia, who stands to the side with her arms
crossed over her chest so tight I'm worried
she's going to cut off circulation.

She looks horrified. "That's like four hundred calories."

She says it like I should know that already.
Like I should be horrified, too.

I glance down at my donut,
at my teeth marks in the dough,
and the aftertaste of sugar on my tongue suddenly turns bitter.

"I'd be careful if I were you."
Kāia pokes me in the soft part of my belly, smirking
as if we're just joking around,

but my sister's never been that funny.

I roll my eyes and take another bite
of the donut
right
in
her
face.

"You worry about you, I'll worry about me,"
I mumble around a mouthful.

Kāia's nose crinkles. "You're so gross."

"Thank you." I smile wide, showing off
the chocolate frosting stuck in my teeth.

At a loss for what to do with her

gross,
            vile,
disgusting,
            calorie-ignorant,
                        donut-possessed sister,

Kāia huffs and puffs around a bit
before stomping off to join our parents.

Only
once
I
am
sure
she can't see

me,

I spit it all out
into my napkin
and dump the rest
of the donut in the trash.

I catch up with my family
just as Mama spots the Tuigamalas
sitting at a table nearby.

The Tuigamalas are a Samoan couple from Waimea,
the same small town that Mama and Dad are from
on the north side of Hawaiʻi Island.

They're Pacific Islander, like us.
Which basically makes us family.

But we're Hawaiian, *not* Samoan.

Yes, it's different.

The Tuigamalas are nice,

so nice
that Mr. Tuigamala always matches his aloha print shirts
with Mrs. Tuigamala's colorful mu'umu'us,

so nice
that Mr. Tuigamala loves to perform silly magic tricks
just to make you laugh,

so nice
that Mrs. Tuigamala always makes sure to ask
before giving you a hug,

so nice
that they always send cards for your birthday
and money for Christmas and baskets of candy for Easter—

 even after Dad tells them to stop
 because you're supposed to be too old
 for stuff like that.

The Tuigamalas are so nice
that you might even
sometimes
secretly
wish
they were your parents
instead.

"Come sit, come sit!"
Mr. Tuigamala insists,
but
when Mama starts toward them—

"We should be getting home," Dad says quietly,
so only we can hear him.

Mama's smile falters briefly (so briefly I almost miss it).
"Next time!" she promises.

Mrs. Tuigamala waves us off. "No worry!"

And as we turn to leave,
Mr. Tuigamala raises a hand to say goodbye.
"You girls be good for your maddah and faddah, yeah?"

Dad returns the gesture as his other hand guides me away.
"Of course, they always are!"

We don't have a big house,
like the mansions near the lake.

Or a small house,
like the apartments behind the grocery store
in town.

We're
somewhere
right
in
the
middle.

It's just enough
for the four of us—

a little cramped kitchen,
a living room with a fireplace,
an office for Dad,
three bedrooms upstairs all clustered together
down a single dark hallway,
and the bathroom that my sister and I
are constantly at war over—

it's an old house.
The walls are thin, and the people are close,
and I
can

hear
everything.

I can hear my sister
through the wall we share between us
and the conversations she has with just herself.

I can hear my father
when he snaps at Mama,
then when he's met with her soft replies.

I can hear my mother
turn off all the lights in her room
and her deep sigh when she finally goes to bed.

And I can hear
when the door to Dad's office opens one more time,
when he switches on all the lights,
when Mama asks him "why,"
which only

sparks

another

fight.

Tonight

it

rains

plunk

plop plop

plunk plunk

drop drop drop drop

plunk plunk plunk plop

plunk plunk plunk plunk plunk

plunk plunk plunk plunk plunk plunk

plunk plunk plunk plunk plunk plunk plunk

drop plunk plunk plunk plunk drop plunk drop

plunk plunk drop plunk plunk plunk plop plunk plop

drop plunk plunk plunk plunk plunk plunk plunk plunk

drop plunk plop plunk plunk plunk plunk plunk plunk plop

plunk plunk plunk plunk plop plunk plunk plunk plunk plunk

plunk plunk plunk plunk plunk plunk plunk plunk plunk drop

plunk plunk drop plunk plunk plunk plunk plunk plunk plunk

plunk plunk plunk plunk plunk plop plop plop plop plop plop

plunk drop plop plop plunk plunk plunk plunk plop plop plop

plunk plunk drop drop plunk plunk plunk plunk plunk plunk

plunk plunk plunk plunk plunk plunk plunk plunk plop

plunk plunk plunk plunk plunk plunk plunk plunk

my own melancholy melody *plop plunk drop*

to back the sound *plop plunk drop*

of Mama and Dad arguing

about me.

January 26

Monday

The meaty aroma
of fried Spam
at the
bottom of
a cast-iron pan
wafts up
the stairs
to wake me.
When I
join Dad in
the kitchen
he hums
to himself
as he
turns over
a bowl of
thinly
sliced
green onion,
oil hissing
when it
hits the pan.
Dad
always makes
fried rice
the day after

yelling
at me.
It's his way
of saying
sorry
without
actually
saying
sorry
at
all.
"Egg on top?"
he asks,
which
translates to
Forgive me?
"Sure,"
I say,
which
translates to
I forgive you, Dad.
I always do.
Don't I?

Kāia drives me to school
because she has to
not because she wants to,
she reminds me as I slide into the passenger seat
fifteen minutes after we were supposed to leave.
"The least you can do"—she checks her mirrors—"is be ready"—
she checks them again—"to go on time."
She triple-checks,

and then I

check

out

as she goes
on
and
on
and
on
(and
on
and
on
and
on).

We go
our separate
ways

the moment
we pull into the student lot.

Kāia beelines for the science wing.

I drag my feet toward the football field,
where Taylor is waiting for me
by the bleachers,

knowing I won't see my sister again
until the day is over
and it's time to go
home.

The dinner table
is quiet tonight,

but it's always quiet.

At least until
Dad asks us about school.

Kāia answers:
"Great."
"Good."
"I got a hundred percent."
"No, that's due next week."
"Yes, I'm already done."

I answer:
"Fine."
"I don't know."
"But *no one* got a good score."
"I don't know when it's due."
"Sure, I'll work on it tonight."

And only once he's satisfied,
we all go back
to being quiet.

January 28

Wednesday

Kāia drags me out of bed this morning
with her own two hands and refuses to leave my room
as I dress in stormy silence.

Of course she was ready for the day
before she came barging in, with her

frizzy black hair tamed into submission
by a blow-dryer,

perfect makeup, done in a way
that looks like she's not even wearing any,

and pristine drill team uniform
in gold, blue, and white
and a big C patch for Captain over her heart.

It's Wednesday.
Spirit day.

Go, Dragons!

Gag.

Hawk Valley, Washington State
pop. 20,000

is your run-of-the mill
mostly white
middle-class
suburban
*meh*hole
about forty-five minutes south of Seattle,
          an hour during rush hour,
and 2,700 miles from Kona.

The weather is *meh* and the people are *meh,*

          but

there is a stretch of road on the way to school

the forest the forest   *that*   the forest
the forest the forest   *slices*   the forest
the forest the forest   *straight*   the forest
the forest the forest   *through*   the forest

                    the forest,

and if you watch the evergreens blur together,
and you stick your hand out the window to feel the wind
rush over your skin,

it feels like flying,   and that's pretty sweet.

February 1

Fourth Sunday in Ordinary Time

After a break for Christmas vacation,
youth group starts back up today, which means

I get to sit with Taylor
and the other teenagers during mass, which means

I don't have to sit with my parents
and pretend to pay attention, which means

I'm seated right behind Damien's
perfect yellow-haired head instead, which *means*

I'm
exactly
where
I'm
supposed
to
be.

What would Jesus do
if he knew
just
how
sexy
he looked up there
behind Father Ambrose?

Bloody,
pained, and
absolutely ripped.

Taylor leans in. "Jake's abs look *just like that.*"

"Our Father who art in heaven," I whisper
with my head still bent in prayer,
"hallowed be thy smoking-hot son."

We erupt in giggles so loud that Sister Tammy—
not a nun,
just a prude—

shushes us,

but that only makes us laugh
harder.

Jacob Li is, indisputably, the hottest guy in our class,
and he asked Taylor to *officially* be his girlfriend
two weeks ago, so Taylor's been feeling
pretty
hot
herself,
too.

Jake isn't Catholic. He's Buddhist.
So mass is the perfect place to gush
about Jake.
Jake's abs.
Jake's eyes.
Jake's—

but now
I'm picturing Jake's face
                    on Jesus's body,
and shame burns hot across my skin.

I'm grateful Taylor doesn't notice.

She's already moved on
to Jake's ass.

Father Ambrose raises his hands.
                    Pew stands slap back into place—
                    crack! crack! crack!

And as I rise
my gaze grazes Jesus's (now Jake's)
ceramic
bloody
abs.

"Turn away from sin," Father Ambrose commands,

so I fold my hands,
close my eyes,
and pretend to turn away.

Youth group is split
into three different factions.

1. The kids who actually take church seriously,
   like Julie Stevens and my sister.
2. The kids who come because they have no choice,
   like Taylor and me.

And of course,

3. The Apostles.

The Apostles
are mostly rich white kids who go to St. Joseph's Preparatory
instead of public school like the rest of us *lowly* nobodies.
I don't know when Taylor and I started calling them the Apostles,
just that it would be weird
if we stopped
now.

The Holy Clique
Tia
Katie
August
Landon
Lola
Brady
Jessie
Garrett
Luke
Abby
Damien (*sigh*) and Damien's older brother,
Derek.   Their fearless leader.

They're just shy of a legitimate Last Supper.

My sister and I don't have much in common,
but we do share a type.

Kāia has shamelessly pined after Derek Miller since,
well, probably since I started shamelessly pining after his brother.

Of course, she's never actually told me this.
I just know where she keeps her journal.

Under the pillowcase is not very original,

nor is it very secure.

When Taylor and I
walk into youth group after mass,
Kāia is already sitting in the middle seat of the front row,

wearing a dark blue sweater
that says YALE in big white block letters across her chest
(even though she hasn't even gotten in yet),

with her own Bible
open on the table in front of her.

So embarrassing.

I pay no attention to her.
Just how she pays no attention to me.

And it occurs to me
for the first time
that maybe she's embarrassed
by me,
too.

The Apostles always
sit in the back of the classroom—

and by classroom
I mean the former daycare room
that still has old toys stacked in the corners collecting dust
and Noah's ark–inspired cartoons faded and forgotten
on the walls—

and today is no exception.

Damien is at the center of the action.
    Chair tilted back on two feet.
    Hands cradling the back of his head.
    Smug grin on his face when August cracks a joke.

"*Stop* staring." Taylor tugs on my elbow.
My defense comes quickly. "I'm *not*."

But
I
totally
am.

My life changed
in fifth grade
when the Miller family
moved from Seattle to Hawk Valley.

Which is crazy lucky for me
because who in their right mind
would move to Hawk Valley?

My parents have obviously never been
in their right minds.

For this
and other reasons.

There are four Miller brothers,
each one year apart
with a name that starts with *D*.

Yeah.
One of those families.

Daniel.
Dawson.
Derek.
Damien.

All tall.
All blond.
All annoyingly hot.

And it didn't take long at all
for me to start daydreaming
about Damien Miller.

So what if I can count the number
of actual conversations we've had
on one hand?

We're
totally
meant
to
be.

Taylor purses her lips,
like she's considering something serious,
until—

"What are you doing?"

Taylor is nearly dragging me toward two open seats
smack
in
the
middle
of Apostles Territory.

"Do you want Damien to finally notice you or what?"
she asks at a volume that is much too loud
for my comfort.

"Stop pulling." I dig in my heels, yet she has the audacity
to look at me like I'm the one acting crazy.
"Why are you doing this to me?"

She sighs. "This is my New Year's resolution."

"To embarrass me into cardiac arrest?"

"To get a boyfriend."

"You have a boyfriend."

Her grip tightens around my wrist.
"No, to get a boyfriend for *you*."

Tia Nelson is staring at me.
Openly.

I'm sure she's just as confused as I am
about how Taylor and I ended up

here

with Damien in the seat to my left
and Tia on the other side of Taylor to my right,
and sweat making my palms slick—

nothing like
profuse perspiration
to add to an already
stressful
situation!

"So, where do you guys go to school?" Tia asks,
skepticism flickering in her blue eyes

like she's forgotten who we are
like we're not worthy of remembering
like she hasn't known us since we were
all toddlers

playing together
at the parish preschool.

Taylor sits back in her chair
like it was put there just for her, unaffected
by Tia's prickly welcome. "Hawk Valley High."

Tia laughs. "That place looks like a prison."

Taylor's face betrays her for only a fraction of a second—
confusion
hurt
then shame—
before she's laughing right along with Tia.

Everyone's conversations end
when Sister Tammy walks into the room
and shushes us all so hard
spittle
flies out of her mouth.

Sister Tammy is only a few years older
than Kāia and the other seniors,
but she loves to act
like she's so much
wiser and
holier
than the rest of us,

just because when Miss Sheila retired—
the former youth group leader
who started the whole program
thirty years ago—
she was the only one who wanted the gig.

Sister Tammy takes her JesusCore aesthetic
so seriously, I often wonder
if she's intentionally messing with us,

because her outfit today is even more
ridiculous than usual

and there's no way she actually wants to look
like a sales rep for Christianity.

Black sweatpants with *John 3:16*
screen-printed across the hip.

A red T-shirt with a huge cross circled by
the words *My Lifeguard Walks on Water.*

A comically large silver crucifix
hanging around her neck that looks
like it was made to ward off vampires.

I snicker under my breath thinking
only Taylor will hear me

but then I catch Tia's eye, and I'm surprised.

Surprised to see her smirk of approval.
Surprised by how good it makes me feel (at first).
Surprised the most
by the sudden knot of guilt
tightening
in my chest.

It's hard to focus
on the Bible verse activity in front of me
when Damien Miller

smells

so

good.

Like sweat and body spray
and *oh my God*
if it's not the most heavenly smell.

I could steep myself in it,

which is why I can't help but take
a long *totally* creepy inhale
when his back is turned to me.

Taylor elbows me in the ribs.
Did you just smell him? she mouths.

But before I can deny it,
Tia interrupts

because maybe
there *is* a God.

"There's a bonfire happening on Friday,"
Tia says, like we are just supposed to know
what that means.

When neither of us responds, she goes on, slowly,
"After the St. Joe's basketball game.
You two should come."

She shrugs like it's no big deal, but
she knows
Taylor knows
I know

this
is
a
huge
deal.

"Sounds fun." Taylor tries to play it cool,
but I know her too well.
    She's one false step from squealing
    like a little kid on Christmas.
"*Right,* Lily?"

It's never bothered me
that Taylor and I have always

floated

right on the edge of

popular
    and outcast,

cool
    and weird,

the in-group
    and the outskirts,

because even if we never
knew where we
belonged exactly,

we knew we belonged together.

Best friends.
                        Forget the rest.

Us
                        against the world,

but—

maybe
it's never bothered me,

but

it bothers her.

Maybe she knows,

maybe she's always known
exactly where she
belongs.

Maybe
it's just me

who hasn't figured
it out.

Maybe she's waiting
for me to catch up.

Maybe she's tired.

Maybe she's finally
had enough.

Maybe

she's finally done
with being

held

back.

"Earth to Lily?"

"Sorry, what was that?"

Taylor is staring at me so hard it looks like
she's trying to communicate with me telepathically—

like we used to when we were kids, convinced
that if we just tried hard enough
we would be able to read
each other's minds.

"Bonfire. Friday. We'll be there?" she prompts me.

"Oh, I mean . . . my dad probably wouldn't let me—"

She cuts me off. "We'll be there," she assures Tia,
who doesn't appear to care either way.

Now I'm the one staring at Taylor,
trying to get a message through,

but all I hear is silence.

February 4

Wednesday

Dad has to take me to school today
on his way in to work,
because Kāia wanted to get to the library early
to study for a history test,
and I was too slow.

He and I don't talk much on the fifteen-minute drive;
instead, we listen to Hawaiian music,

a playlist of his favorite artists like

Keali'i Reichel
Israel Kamakawiwoʻole
The Brothers Cazimero
and Mākaha Sons,

who are some of my favorites, too.

I start out humming,
then mumbling,
then singing outright,
and eventually Dad joins in with me.

Like nimble fingers interlacing thin strips of lauhala
our voices weave together into something beautiful and intricate,
and it feels like the most honest conversation
we've had in a while.

Memory

Ten Years Ago

Early in the morning before he goes to work,
I hear my father singing in Hawaiian.

I try to form my mouth around his words
to mimic the way his ʻiʻi tremors so beautifully.

This is the moment I decide
I am going to be a singer,

just like him.

February 6

Friday

Texts

9:08 p.m.

Taylor: When are you coming over?

Me: ????

Taylor: For the bonfire?

Taylor: Come soon please

Taylor: I need you to do my eyeliner before we leave

9:30 p.m.

Taylor: Hello????

Me: You know I can't go

Taylor has always struggled with the word
no.
Even though
I've told her
every day this week.
No, I can't go to the bonfire.
No, my dad would never let me.
No, I'm not going to ask.
No, the answer is still
no.

Taylor: Come ON Lily
Me: *Typing . . .*
Taylor: Don't make me come over there!!
Taylor: Yes, that is a threat
Taylor: DAMIEN IS LITERALLY GOING TO BE THERE

A compelling argument.

Me: *Typing . . .*
Me: Fine.
Me: I'll ask.

Mama
sits at her vanity
using her fingers
to lift the skin at her temples
                    up
          up
up

and she is a perfect blend
of Bachan and Grandpa.

Delicate almond-shaped eyes.
Thick curly hair.
Thoughtful lips.
Cheekbones only models have.

"Mama?"

She finally notices me standing there
in old flannel pajamas that are a little too short
          and a little too tight.

"Yes?"

I swallow. "Do you think . . ." The end of my question
fades to silence as I try to muster up some nerve.
"Do you think I could go . . ."

Come on, Aouli.

". . . to a party?"
She turns around, eyebrows raised.
"You want to go to a party?"

Yes?
No.
Maybe I don't.
But maybe I do!
Or maybe I just want the freedom
to make the choice
for myself.

Mama sighs out a long, tired breath.
"You would have to ask Dad."
Which translates to *I'm not allowed to make that decision.*

"Can you ask him?" I hope. "For me?"
Which translates to *I'm scared he will get mad at me.*

"You know I can't." She turns away.
Which translates to *I'm scared, too.*

Dad's office
is a shrine to himself.
The Honorable Christopher Kaimana Smith.
    Degrees and
    awards and articles
    are his only decorations.
All hung in chronological order.
Neat. Organized. Not a single thing out of place.
A perfect timeline
of his perfect life.

Dad sits behind his desk
with his glasses low
at the tip of his nose as he reads
something on his computer.

"Dad?"

He takes his glasses off.
He crosses his arms tight.
The walls close in.
Degrees and
awards and
articles
all
look
down

at

me.

Mouth set.

Gaze impatient.

"What, Aouli?"

But I'm already out the door.

"Sorry, Dad."

I'm already shaking my head. "Never mind, Dad."

Don't know why I even bothered, Dad,

when you've never *ever*

been willing

to just

give

me

a

chance.

Why would you start now?

Texts

10:01 p.m.

Me: Sorry my dad said no

Taylor: Oh my goddd

Taylor: Lily!!!!

Taylor: Just sneak out

Taylor: It's not that hard

10:10 p.m.

Taylor: Lily????????????

White kids

are
always
sneaking
out
and
they
think
that
makes
them
the
shit
but
really
they
just

don't

have

a

super

freaking

scary-ass

Hawaiian

dad

like

me.

I find my sister in her room,
which is thick with the smell of vanilla perfume.

She thinks it makes her smell important,

but it just makes her smell
like a cupcake.

I catch her staring at herself in the mirror
atop her dresser.

She is beautiful. Just like Mama.

Even with the skin between her brows all scrunched up
and her lips pressed hard into a thin, disappointed line
and her hands on her hips pushing ininin.

Does she think that with enough pressure
and sheer willpower
she can make her stomach disappear altogether?

"Kāia?"

She looks up.
Not at me.
Through me.
Like I am a ghost that won't stop
haunting her.

"What?"

"I . . . there's this . . ." I wring my hands together
until my fingers start to ache.

Kāia groans.

"Just

spit

it

out,

Lily."

So I shut the door,
and I
spit
it out.

"There's a party.
A bonfire.
St. Joe's kids. Taylor's going, too.
I asked Mama, then I tried—
well, never mind.
I was wondering,
maybe, if you wouldn't mind . . .
You see . . .
I really
really
really want to go.
At least, I think I want to go?
I want to be able to go."
I step toward her. "What do you think—"

She sinks out of reach,

and I abandon the end of my question
at the tip of my tongue
to suffocate on the stench of vanilla perfume

hanging heavy

between

us.

Kāia

My sister is everything
I am not.

Quiet as the flap
of a butterfly's wings.

Gentle as ukulele
on the ear.

Soft
pliable
obedient
as any good girl

is supposed to be.

I am not
her.

I am not

soft
pliable
obedient
but

loud as the beat
of a wave against rock.

Harsh as the bite
of blessed Sunday wine.

Hard
unmoving
unforgiving
as we were taught

not to be.

As I was expected
as I was molded
as I was formed

not
to be.

But like the

loud
harsh
hard
strike

of whatever I am

I remain
unmoved.

I remain
unmoved
still

in the doorframe
of my sister's room

waiting for her
to stop
looking

at her hands
at her waist
at her sad
perfect
face

to stop
looking

through
the reflection of
me

in the mirror
and to just
just
just

look
at
me.

I need her to see
that I need
her

to be my sister
now
for once
for the first time ever.

I need
her

to tell me
to go
to be free.

I
need
her.

"Girls, what are you doing?"
Dad opens the door before we have a chance to respond.
His eyes scan the room, then our faces,

searching for anything
that isn't as it should be.

"Why aren't you both asleep?" he asks,

but I hear the real warning in his tone:
Bed.
Now.
Don't make me tell you again.

"We were just saying good night, Dad."
The lie flies without a thought,
before Kāia has a chance to tell on me.

His lips tighten.
He shakes his head.
He starts to leave.

Then he looks at me. Just at me.

Like he knows something.
Like he knows somehow that I considered sneaking out.
Like I already messed up.
Like he's already found me

guilty.

"We should go to bed, Aouli,"
Kāia says once he is gone,

her own warning
hiding behind
her words.

"But—"

She turns
her back
on
me.

"Go to bed."

I go
to bed
to try to be

what is expected,

soft
gentle
quiet.

As I fall asleep
I try to pray
for real.

I fold my hands
and close my eyes,

not to fool someone
into thinking

I am praying
but to try

and fool myself
into thinking

I'm the kind
of girl who prays

for real.

Dear God,
I am sick

and tired

of this

cage

that's

always

been

too

small.

Amen.

Memory

Thirteen Years Ago

My father's bedtime stories
never have happy endings.

"From the sky came the crow, 'Alalā.
Our 'aumakua born of the wind.
Our ancestor,
whose voice could be heard across
the island,
                from the mountains
                                down to the sea.
But she sang her song
alone.
Her family was taken,

and so she searched
for another like her,
but before she could
find them
she was
stolen
from
the
sky."

"Who took 'Alalā?" I ask him,
from under the protection of his arm.

We sit together, beneath a ceiling
littered with a hundred glow-in-the-dark stars.

"Hunters."

"Why?" I ask, because I am still at the age
when *why* is my favorite word to bother
my parents with.

Dad sighs deeply,
like he hates the question,
like he hates that I asked,
like he hates that he has to be the one

to tell me the truth.

"They wanted her wings."

February 7

Saturday

hundreds

of *caw!*

crows

flock

caw!

outside

the house

circling *caw!*

diving

caw!

caw! swimming

caw!

through

the air

caw!

singing

their

caw!

morning *caw!*

songs

"Crows freak me out."
Kāia eyes the flock through the window
over the kitchen sink,

a spoonful of yogurt hovering
halfway between the bowl in her hand
and her mouth.

I play with my own yogurt,
without ever actually taking a bite.
"I don't know. I find them kind of
beautiful."

She frowns.
"You freak me out, too."

But I don't hear her really,

all

I

hear

is

the

music.

Sundays
are
for
God, but
Saturdays are for
Aunty ʻEhu's house,
which feels a lot like church
is supposed
to feel,
I think.

My Aunty Kōnane Smith
is my late grandfather's sister
and the coolest person I know.

She was named Kōnane after the moonlight
shining brightly on a dark night,
    but everyone calls her ʻEhu, the nickname
    my grandfather gave her when they were both little,
    for the reddish hue of her hair.

Aunty ʻEhu never married or had kids.
"Too much trouble," she's always said.
    "I'm enough as it is," she's never failed to add.

She moved to Washington from Hawaiʻi when I was ten,
to be closer to us.

"You two are my favorites," she whispers
to Kāia and me whenever our cousins are around,
holding me with one hand
and tugging Kāia close with the other.

Over the years, it's become tradition to spend Saturdays
at her house,

a beacon for Hawaiians
who've found themselves
too far from home,
some of them family by blood,
others by the heart,

all of us
finding a place to land
in Aunty 'Ehu's warm arms.

Family Lū'au Rules:
Leave your slippahs at the front.
Come in, come, come, come, come.
No mind the dog, he like to bark.
Go kiss your aunties hello.
Go kiss your uncles hello.
Go grab one beer from the cooler for me,
and make sure the lid shut good.
Go kiss your cousins hello. Hele, hele.

Tell your aunty about that history project.
Tell your uncle about that science fair.
Tell your cousin about that one guy,
        you know *the guy*.
        He'll think it's funny.
        No be shy about it.
Don't let the hot air out.
Don't track mud into my kitchen.
Go grab one other beer for your uncle, too.
Make a plate, make a plate, make a plate!
But go help your cousin make one plate
        for the baby first.
Tell your cousin to turn that music down.
Tell her turn it up again. Nobody can hear!
Go bring one wine opener from the kitchen.
        You like try open it yourself? Ha!
Go check on the babies.
Go ask if they need help in the kitchen.
Go make sure the car is locked.
Go hang out with your cousins. They miss you.
Go grab the others. We got to pray.
Go hula with your aunties.
Go sing with your faddah. He would love that.
Go, honey girl.
You kiss everybody hello, yeah?
Good.

My family comes alive

at Aunty 'Ehu's house—

Kāia lounging on the couch without a crease
of worry on her face, talking with her mouth full
of fried wontons and earthy laughter.

Mama sitting around the table with the women,
basking in the brief sun shining through the windows,
glowing, glowing, glowing.

Dad speaking pidgin without fear,
every word erupting from his soul, singing
every time a Braddah Iz song comes on.

I come alive here, too,

chasing my little cousins around the yard and back
into the house, through the kitchen, past my aunties
calling after me.

"Eh!"

"Cut it out!"

"You bettah be careful, girl!"

Picking each kid up one by one, swinging them in the air,
so that they can know how it feels
to fly.

Stretched long
across the couch, I look out
the window to watch
the sun dip lower
and lower
until
it disappears completely
behind the snowcapped peaks
of the Olympics. And soon,
the sky is pitch-black.
No moon.
No stars.
Just rippling clouds to drape
the world in the most
luxurious fabric.

The goodbyes begin,
and I pretend to sleep

like I am seven
instead of seventeen,

hoping to steal just five more minutes
of this peace

tucked into the corner
of this couch that's older than me,
where the fabric is threadbare and soft,

five more minutes in this house
that smells sweet like nānū,

five more minutes wrapped up tight
in this chiffon sky.

"Aouli." Dad's hand is surprisingly gentle
on my arm.

I squeeze my eyes shut
and try my best to appear asleep,
so that he has no choice
but to leave me be.

"Aouli," he says again, but this time his voice
is stiff. My name a command. "It's time to go."

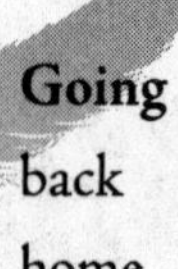

is always
the worst
part of
Saturday.

February 15

Sixth Sunday in Ordinary Time

Turns out
missing the bonfire on Friday
meant missing out on inside jokes
and crazy stories I'll never know the ending to
and the exact moment Tia went from not knowing
who Taylor was
to being Taylor's
new
best
friend.

I'm up way too late thinking
about Taylor
and Tia
and the stupid bonfire
I should have been at,

so late that when Dad retires from working
sometime past midnight in his office,
I'm awake to hear him
when he starts to sing
in the shower.

And it's his voice
that finally
lulls me to sleep.

Dream

The air is dry
and cool

as the sunset colors
the bare slopes of Mauna Loa
gold.

A crow soars above,
singing
singing
singing
singing.

February 16

Monday

Taylor ditches lunch
to make out with Jake in his car,
and I have music stuck in my head,

so I retreat to the library by myself
and find a seat alone in the back.

I slip my song journal out of my backpack—
the cover of which is blue, stained, and well-worn
from years of use.
It was a gift from Mama,
a place for all the songs in my head to go.

But they aren't really songs,
just lyrics
aching
for a melody that I don't know how to write.

I like to flip through the pages slowly,
seeing how much I've changed over the years,

how my handwriting has sharpened
and how my words have found shape,
evolving from stray clusters to neat lines.

I hold my pen loosely between my fingers
and start sifting through the mess in my head,
hoping it will begin
                    to make sense
                                        on the page.

February 18

Ash Wednesday

When Taylor sees me walk into the narthex
behind my family she squeals and takes off running
through the growing crowd to hug me,
          knocking the breath out of me on impact.

"Geez." I hug her back. "Good to see you, too."

          And even though I sound sarcastic,
          I really mean it.

"I have to tell you something . . ." She trails off, grinning
so big she's going to split her lip.

She leans in close, dropping her voice low,
so only I can hear her.

"Jake.

And.

I.

Had.

Sex!"

"Shut. *Up.*"

"Quiet, quiet—" she shushes me, but it's no use
because we're already causing a scene.
Jumping up and down, holding on to each other
for dear life.

We speak at the same time:

"I couldn't wait to tell you."

"I have to know everything."

She sputters. "It will be like you were *there.*"

I groan. "Oh, gross." But it's not long
until I'm laughing again.

"I haven't told anyone else." She smiles at me conspiratorially
and all my internal agonizing from the past few days,
worrying she was about to ditch me for Tia,
suddenly seems so silly.

"Really?"

She rolls her eyes. "Of course. Just you

and Tia."

Ah.

Not

so

silly

after

all.

"Aouli."

I freeze.

Dad's voice is quiet. Calm,
even. But I know
better.

I see it

on his face when I muster up the courage
to look at him.

Disappointment.

Taylor's voice is distant in my ear. "I'll text you."
Then she's gone.

Mama watches me. Silent.

Kāia keeps her distance. Worried, probably,
that if she stands too close
she might catch Dad's wrath, too.

"We're at church," he spits. "Behave." Behave. Behave. Behave.

Behave.
Behave.
Behave.

Behave. Be—
soft
gentle
quiet.

Father Ambrose
swipes his thumb through ash to mark
my skin.

"Repent your sins, my daughter."

There are too many, my Father. My sins stick
and cling just like this ash.

Father Ambrose swipes his thumb through ash
once more to mark my dad.

"Repent your sins, my son."

What are his sins, Father?

His ash doesn't stick or cling
like mine.

It falls.
It falls.
It falls.
It falls.

It falls.

It falls.

It falls.

It falls.

It falls.

I

t

f

a

l

l

s.

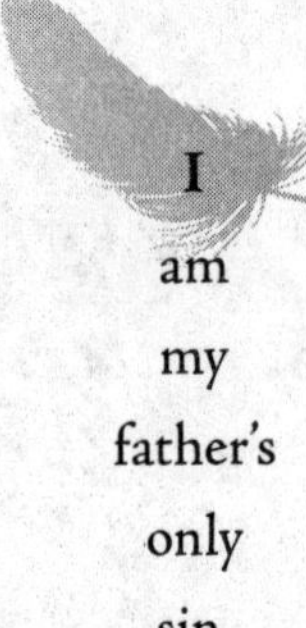

I
am
my
father's
only
sin.

Memory

Nine Years Ago

I always ached
to know my father better,
but only now do I decide to go searching
for paths to his heart.

That's how I find myself
at his desk—

I take care
to slide the drawer out
slowly
preciously
like it is
something holy,
something sacred,
something I know is not meant for me.

Gum.
Reading glasses.
A pack of cigarettes.
Pennies and nickels and dimes
all throughout like confetti.
Each item is an artifact
and I, its excavator.

I inspect closely,
holding each piece

of my father
gingerly—

and there
tucked away
and hidden

is a card, and inside it reads:

I love you

in small, slender handwriting.

And it feels like I have come across
something that is not precious
nor sacred
nor holy,
but something haunted,
something

not

meant

to

be

disturbed.

Family time
is a lot like dinnertime.
Quiet
except
for the dull
buzz of the television.

We only have cable, because Dad is stubborn.
So tonight we're watching
the regularly scheduled
programming of
Mama
flip
flip
flip
flip
flip
flip
flip
flip
flip
flip
flip
flip
flip
flipping
through the channels, unable
to ever settle
on one.

Kāia fell asleep.

I'm not far from drifting off, too.
We're squished together on the couch, neither of us
willing to make space for the other, determined to take up
as much room as we can for ourselves. I jam my elbow into her,
scooch my hips, and smash her against the seat, but her body
sinks heavy into me, pinning me closer to her than
I've been in a long long time.

Dad is on his phone,
which is annoying
because he yells at me if *I'm* on *my* phone in the living room,

but the rules never apply to him.

Kāia starts to snore,
Mama continues to flip,
and I read over Dad's shoulder
because I'm nosy

and
I'm
still
looking
for
paths.

Texts

11:15 p.m.

Dad: Flight lands at noon in Spokane.

Her: I'll be there to pick you up.

Her: I miss you.

Dad: I miss you, too.

Her: I can't wait to see you.

Her: I love you.

"There's nothing to watch."

Mama gives up.
"What do you guys want to watch?"
  I don't answer.
  I can't.
Because Dad doesn't see me looking.
Because I'm supposed to be asleep.
Because Dad is still texting, and my heart
is expanding
in my chest
threatening
threatening
threatening
to break
right
through
the
bone—

Dad: I love you too, Gina.

Five words
to break
my
heart
open.
Pop! Pop! Pop! Pop! Pop!
Mama sighs.
She turns off the TV.
The screen goes dark
and all that is left
is the blue glow
of Dad's phone,
a lantern
to illuminate
the path through
the hole in my chest.

The path
is a
name
a safe
name
that is
gentle
on your
tongue
and
easy
on the
mouth
a name
that is
sweet
but
not
too
sweet
a name
that
doesn't
scream
or call
attention
to itself
a name
that does

not bite
or snarl
or snap
a nice
name
that
won't
ever
be
said
wrong
Gina
Gina
Gina
Gina
Gina
Gina
Gina
Gina
Gina
Gina
Gina
Gina
Gina
Gina
Gina
Gina
Gina
Gina

Gina
Gina
Gina
Gina
Gina
Gina
Gina
Gina
Gina
Gina
Gina
Gina
Gina
Gina
Gina
Gina
Gina
Gina
Gina
Gina
Gina
Gina
a name
that
sticks
with
you
years
later
when

you
realize
it was
her name
scratching
at your
skin a
perfect
name
in small
and slender
handwriting
I love you,
Gina.

Kāia sighs in her sleep
and curls closer into me, flinging her arm
around me and drawing me in.

I hold on tight,
unsure of what would happen
to me if I let go
now.

February 19

Thursday After Ash Wednesday

"Why are you staring at me?"
Kāia asks, sitting across from me at the dining table
that's always been a little too big for this tiny kitchen.

I could tell her.
I could tell her right now.
I could tell her all about
Gina
Gina
Gina
Gina
Gina.

Mama is getting ready for work.
Dad left thirty minutes ago.
I could tell Kāia

everything.

"Never mind."

Never mind.
Never mind.
Never mind.
Never mind.
Never mind.
Never mind.
Never mind.
Never mind.
Never mind.
Never mind.
Never mind.
Never mind.
Never mind.
Never mind.
Never mind.
Never mind.
Never mind.
Never mind.
Never mind.
Never mind.
Never mind.
Never mind.
Never mind.

I can't.
I can't say it
out loud.

On the drive to school,
trees blur,
rain
hits
the
window,

little worlds
in little drops

to watch me
carve the name
with the tip
of my nail into the flesh
of my palm.

I need to get it out
get it out
get it
out
Gina
Gina
Gina
Gina
Gina
Gina
Gina
Gina
Gina

until
my hand
starts to hurt,

until
the skin
starts to bleed,

until
Kāia is barking at me to
"Get out, you're going to be late."

Taylor wasn't waiting for me
by the bleachers like usual, so now I'm barreling
down the hallway.

The palm of my hand stings, but it will heal.

It's small.
It's insignificant.

It's nothing.

Nothing compared to the hole in my chest.

I need to find Taylor.
I need my best friend.

When I turn the corner toward our lockers,
I see her copper hair,
                    a beacon of safety
                    calling me back to shore.

Then I see Jake.

Jake, who is curled around my best friend
like an overgrown vine.
I can't tell her about Gina Gina Gina Gina now.
          Not in front of Jake.

"Hey!" Taylor waves me down, but I don't know
what to do or how I am supposed to act.

So I try to go through the motions.
Open my locker.
Busy myself.
Look for something I don't need.

"Did you finish the calc homework?" she asks,
oblivious to the hole in my chest.

                    The big-ass bleeding hole!

I mutter, "Yeah."

"Can I copy?" she asks. *"Please?"*
She presses her hands together,
pleading,

begging,
praying.

Jake adjusts and twines himself closer.
I shut the locker.

Can't she see I'm bleeding?

Can't she see—

Taylor holds her hand out.
So I pass my math notebook over.
Mumble an excuse for why I need to leave.
Turn on my heel to depart as the first bell rings.
Leave a ravine of blood
blood
blood
blood
blood
blood
blood
blood
blood
blood
blood
flowing
in my
wake.

There's this show on the Food Network
that I

secretly

love to watch.

Crazy Cuisines with Bud Martini.

Today, after school, I get really emotional watching
Bud try weird foods in Tucson.

Mama doesn't notice.
Her eyes are on Bud,
on her phone,
on her hands as she rubs lotion into her skin
over and over until it is all slick and wet.

Her eyes are everywhere
except
on
me.

I wish Bud Martini was my dad.
He seems like a good one.
He seems like he never cheated on his wife,
but I have to make sure.

So I look up *Bud Martini cheating scandal*
just in case.

Turns out he's not a cheater, but he might be homophobic,

which really sucks because it seems to me
that everyone's dad is turning out to be something
they're not supposed to be.

And now I have to find a new fake dad.
And a new show to watch when I'm sad.

"Mama?"

She doesn't hear me.

"Mama?"

Or maybe,

"Mama?"

she doesn't want to.

"Mama—"

She sighs, "What is it, Aouli?" and yet,
she still doesn't look at me.

It's Gina
Gina
Gina
Gina
Gina
Gina
Gina
Gina
Gina
Gina
Gina Gina Gina. "It's nothing."

It's not like you would hear me,
anyways.

February 21

Saturday After Ash Wednesday

We shed
our outer shells
and m e l t
into Aunty 'Ehu's open arms.

"A o u l i," she croons
my name soft and smooth
and safe
on her tongue.

Aunty ʻEhu always has everything we need.

T e n d e r hands
to tether my mother to something solid.

L a u g h t e r
to remind my father where his heart is.

K i n d words
to keep away the doubts that linger over my sister.

Aunty ʻEhu takes my hand last
to search my face for what I need.

I wait, but
I fear
I need too much.

And when she looks at me, I know
she sees it.

The hole in my chest
that even she
cannot
fill.

Texts

10:33 p.m.

Taylor: Tia's having a bunch of people over tonight!

Taylor: you should comeeeeeeee

Taylor: pleasseeeeee

Taylor: WAIT

Taylor: Let me guess?

Taylor: *in whiny ass Lily voice*

Taylor: I cantttttttttt

Taylor: my dad is too scawyyyyyyyyy

Me: I'm in

Taylor: SHUT UP

Me: I can meet you at your house in 30?

10:37 p.m.

Taylor: YES YES YES

Taylor: Sorry I got distracted

Taylor: Thought I saw PIGS FLYING OUTSIDE MY WINDOW

Fuck my dad.

He doesn't
get to make me feel
like I'm not good enough
anymore

for wanting to fly
for wanting
to be
free.

I don't think
before I open the window,
set the screen aside,
feel the night air kissing my cheeks,
trust Mahina shining in the sky

full and robust,
singing
promises

that the fall isn't far
for someone with wings

so

I

jump—

Part Two

Watch and pray so that you will not fall into temptation.
The spirit is willing, but the flesh is weak.
Matthew 26:41

but

I

fall
fall

fall

fall

fall

fall

fall

fall

fall

fall—

how foolish
of
me
to forget

I was not

made

for

soaring.

The floodlights snap on.
I'm in the grass
with my face up to the sky, but

I can't see the moon
anymore.

My ankle is throbbing,
but the hole in my chest

hurts the most, blood
gushing from that place,

soaking into the soil,
and I worry,

what terrible things
will grow from this hurt?

Dad is there first.
A mix of emotions flash
across his face.

Surprise.
Worry.
The hint of a path.
Anger.
Anger.
Anger.
Anger.

"What the hell are you doing?"
He drags me up.

Mama comes running out
of the house, but only to watch

as I am made to stand there
in the cold, until I am in tears,

until my back aches, until I've dug
my fingernails into my palms

so deep I've left crescent dents
in my skin,

until Dad is red in the face, until
he gets in the last word, until

Mama's silence has grown so big,

I've forgotten she's there
at all.

February 22

First Sunday of Lent

The doctor says
it's just a sprain.

The doctor says
there's no cause
for concern.

The doctor says
it will heal soon
enough.

But, Doctor,
what about this hole
in my chest?

I'm bleeding!
I'm bleeding!
I'm bleeding!

But no one listens.
No one hears
me.

My punishment.
Grounded
for three weeks.

No phone.
No friends.
No freedom.

Only home.
Only school.
Only church.

Only cages.

Kāia and I are alone in the car, waiting
for Mama and Dad to head to church

because a sprained ankle and one hour of fitful sleep
isn't a good enough excuse to miss Sunday mass.

Kāia looks like an angel this morning
in a pink dress and a soft white sweater,
and I look like hell
in a pair of the itchiest black tights,
a wrinkly blue dress that doesn't quite match,
and running shoes—
the only shoes that fit around
the bulk of my new ankle brace.

I am a Portrait of a Sad Girl,
all framed in frizzy black hair hanging long
on either side of my face.

I catch my sister watching me
                                        out of the corner of her eye.

"Stop looking at me like that."

She rolls her eyes but looks away. "Like what?"

Like I'm broken, sister.

I curl away from her to rest
my head on the cool glass of the window.

"Nothing. Never mind."

Taylor thinks my sprained ankle
is
so
hilarious
she refuses to stop talking about it.

Even after I ask her to,
she waves me off. "But it's *too* good, Lil."

We're sitting with the Apostles
            because that's just what we do now, I guess,
waiting for youth group to start, and *God*,
I've never so anxiously awaited Sister Tammy's arrival.

"She literally jumped out of her window.
Just poof!" Taylor throws her arms wide like wings,
and the place where my heart used to be
aches.

Tia, Damien, and the others
are all laughing, and it feels
a lot like I'm being
laughed
at.

Damien shakes my shoulder,
rattling me back and forth. "You're *crazy*, Smith.
Who knew?"

            I should be soaring.

Damien Miller just touched me.
But it was rough and uninvited, the way
he jostled me so hard like I'm one of his *bros*.

Damien Miller just talked to me.
But he called me crazy like he meant it
and used my last name like that's something
we just always do.

I should be flying high,

but I've never felt so low.

"You have to tell them the whole story,"
Taylor presses me, making me regret telling her anything
at all. *"Please."*

I leave out a few details.
I don't tell them about the way Dad screamed at me
until I sobbed so hard I couldn't breathe.

I don't tell them about Mama's silence,
the way she let him

hurt me.

I don't tell them about the moment that I thought

I

could

actually

fly.

When I'm done,
once they're finished
with me, Tia and Taylor turn to each other
to debrief last night's party, and

I cease to exist
in their world

while they whisper with their backs
to me in a way that makes me
long
for my best friend.

Dear God,

How can you
feel so far away
from someone

sitting
right next
to you?

Amen.

I catch most
of their conversation

because Tia isn't that good at whispering.

"So." Her eyebrows waggle like a cartoon villain's.
"What did you think of him?"

"So. Hot." Taylor fans herself. "He's new?"

"Yeah, his family just moved here." Tia sighs
like she's already dreaming up
        a big church wedding,
        two kids,
        and a golden retriever.

"I mean, it sucks for him since he's a senior," she adds.

Taylor giggles. "But good for you?"

"G*reat* for me."

My thoughts and prayers to whoever this dreamboat is.

He's going to need them.

"I'm going to sit up front,"
I interrupt suddenly. "To elevate my ankle,"
and to hoard what is left of my dignity.

Taylor glances up at me slowly,
like she forgot I was right next to her
in the first place. "Oh. Okay."

"Sorry—"

but

her back is already turned
to me
once more.

I look away, quick
to hide
the tears
stupid tears
that prickle

at the corners
of my eyes, only
to come
face
to
face with—

Kāia.

She's staring at me.
Sympathy flickering
in her eyes, there
then
gone
in
a
second.

I'm all alone
in the first row
feeling sorry for myself
with my ankle resting on the chair next to me,

when Sister Tammy comes in wearing a T-shirt
that says *Jesus Saves, Bro.*

"Take one and pass it back!" She hands me a stack of half sheets.
"I am going to give you five minutes to silently brainstorm
what you want to give up for Lent."

She smiles at me wide. "Lily! What a pleasant surprise
to have you up in the front for a change," she remarks,
more sarcastic than genuine.
"Happy to see you taking the start of the holy season so *seriously*."

(Bite me.)

Name: Aouli Smith
Directions: Finish the sentence!

For Lent, I am giving up . . .

~~donuts~~
~~traitorous best friends~~
~~bitchy sisters~~
~~dads~~
my will to live!!!!

Halfway through
what is starting to feel
like the longest hour of my life

a boy I've never seen before appears
in the doorway,

causing everyone's heads to turn and look
at the same time.

He's dressed like he went to mass.
Navy pants, collared shirt, loafers.
But he didn't sit with the rest of us up front.

I would have noticed.

Everything about him is polished and neat
except for the black waves that keep falling
into his eyes.

He's tall and broad-shouldered, and he stands
like he knows his size, like he doesn't want
to get in anyone's way.

And his skin, a deep brown, is the same
warm shade as Aunty 'Ehu's. Perennially rich.

He takes a step into the classroom, sliding
an ukulele from under his arm to
the front of his stomach.

Something to shield himself with, perhaps.

> The wood body is painted with flowers
> I recognize from my tūtū's garden back in Waimea.
>
> Bunches of plumeria.
> Garlands of pīkake.
> Proud stalks of pua manu.

"Sorry I'm late," he says to Sister Tammy.
But he doesn't sound sorry. Not really.

And that makes me smile
for the first time
all day.

Sister Tammy waves him toward her.
"Come in! The more the merrier!"

> But if you ask me, she sounds
> pretty miffed about being interrupted.

"You can take this seat." She gestures
to the chair
beside
me,

the one she failed
to notice I'm using
to elevate my ankle.

"Next to Lily."

At that moment,
our gazes meet,
and then
I see

the most peculiar thing:

stars

sparkling in his eyes.

His eyes
are bright
beaming

stars
that shine

to lead
a lost soul

through
the unforgiving

thrash
of the sea.

Star eyes
that see

the dark
skies

plaguing
me

to make me
a galaxy.

Star Eyes
is
the
most
beautiful
boy
I've
ever
seen.

Our first conversation.

Star Eyes: I can grab another chair—?

Me: It's fine.

Star Eyes: Really, I can.

Me: Really, it's fine.

Star Eyes: What happened to your ankle?

Me: I don't think I want to talk about it.

Star Eyes: That's okay.

Me: Are you sure?

Star Eyes: Of course.

Me:

Star Eyes:

Me: You need to write down what you're giving up.

Star Eyes: For what?

Me: For Lent.

Star Eyes: Yeah, I'm probably not going to do that.

Me: Really?

Star Eyes: Yeah.

Me: Why?

Star Eyes: There's nothing I'm willing to live without.

Me: That's cool.

Star Eyes: What are you giving up?

Me: A lot of things.

Star Eyes: Why?

Me: There's a lot I'm willing to live without.

Star Eyes: Can I ask you something?

Me: Sure.

Star Eyes: Are you Hawaiian?

Star Eyes: Because I am, too.

I don't know
what to say at first. "How did you—?"

"Well, are you?"

"Yes, but—"

He beams. "I knew it."

What he doesn't say,
but his star eyes tell me,

is that it's not hard
to figure out

when someone was born
of the same sky
of the same sea
of the same people

as you.

He laughs,
jostling me slightly with his elbow,
gently though,
like we're longtime friends,
and that nanosecond of
contact

is enough
to shock me back to life.

"I'm just playing with you,"
he says quietly, kindly,
as if we're sharing a secret.
"My dad told me to look for
the only other Hawaiian kids.
We know your Aunty 'Ehu."

Ah.
And it all starts
to make sense.

"What's your name?" he asks.

I'm silent.

Why am I not answering his question?
His very, very, very easy question?
Did I forget my name?

It's possible.

"Aouli," I say finally. "My name is Aouli."

I tell him my real name, instead
of my nickname

because it feels overwhelmingly important

that he know who I really am
right from the start.

He smiles.

The world expands.

"Like the big blue sky?" he asks.

I nod.

"I'm Nalu."

I'm not fluent in ʻŌlelo Hawaiʻi,
but I know enough to know his name.

"Like the big blue sea?"

His smile brightens,
and for a moment, neither of us speaks—

"Aouli." He says my name without
anything else
before it
or after.

He says it like it's complete,
like it's full,

like it's perfect all on its own,
and in his mouth,
it is.

"And I'm Kāia."
I jump in my seat.

I swear to *God*.

Nalu turns around in his chair
to greet my sister. "Oh. Hey!"

She holds out her hand.
"I'm the other Hawaiian."
And then he humors her by actually shaking it.

"Now you've met all two of us," I mutter.

He laughs,

what a sound
what a sound
what a sound
what a sound
what a *sound*,

it's music.

Sister Tammy claps to get our attention.
"Okay, my lambs of God!
That's all we have for today!"

Nalu is already up, ukulele at the ready
like he's going to play a song on his way out.

"I like your uke." The words rush out of my mouth
in a moment of desperation

because I am not ready for him to leave
just yet.

He glances at it. "Thanks."

"The art is sick."

"I know." He grins.

"Who painted it?"

"Uh." His smile drops and suddenly I'm panicking
because I said something wrong,
but I don't know why it was wrong.

Why
why
why
why
why could I not just have kept my mouth shut?

"My mom, actually."

I'm scrambling for what to say next,
but he's already starting to go.

"I have to get out of here, but, uh, I'll see you around . . ."
A hint of a smile returns to his face.
"Aouli, like the big blue sky."

He's gone.
The room has mostly emptied.
Taylor must have left with Tia,
I only just noticed.
"Are you coming?" Kāia's waiting for me,
but I'm stuck in my chair.

My mind is whirling because there's still Damien,
a constant in my life like cloud cover,

but now there's this boy
with galaxies in his eyes—

a shooting star
I never saw coming.

February 23

Lenten Monday

Mama and Dad are making dinner in the kitchen
while I pretend to do my homework at the dining table.

". . . Stanley is nice," Mama says, carrying on
a conversation I hadn't been paying attention to,

but Dad is more focused on chopping garlic
than on talking. "Mm-hmm."

Mama leans against the counter. "And his kids
are so sweet. They just started at St. Joseph's Prep."

Dad remains bent over the chopping board. "Sure."

Chop! *Chop!* *Chop!*
Chop! *Chop!* *Chop!* *Chop!*

"What are their names again?"
And I want to ask Mama why she keeps trying.

"Keala." *Chop! Chop! Chop! Chop—* "And Nalu."

I drop my pencil,

scramble to pick it up.

"How do you know them?"
I don't think before asking,
my specialty.

Dad looks up.
Eyes narrow.
Always suspicious.

"They just moved from Kona," Mama explains.
"Uncle Stanley's mother is good friends with Aunty 'Ehu."

"Oh." I try to appear uninterested, nodding slowly

like I
actually
really
totally
don't
care
at
all.

"Try to be friends with Nalu, you and Kāia," Mama suggests,
unaware that I'm no longer in the room with them,

but somewhere up in the stars.

"Aouli?"

"What?"

The stars start to fade, and I fall

back down to Earth.

"Don't say *what,*" Dad scolds,
right as Mama says, "Did you hear me?"

I return to my homework. "Yeah. I mean, *yes.*"

"Uncle Stanley told us Nalu will be joining youth group; was he there yesterday?"

"Yes."

"So you met him?"

"Kind of."

"Try be nice to him, yeah?" Mama sighs.
"It's been a hard year for his family.

His mother passed away."

***That's* why**
my conversation with Nalu ended
the way it did.

The sudden realization
followed immediately by the guilt
is enough to make me so nauseous

that I don't hear anything else
Mama says.

February 24

Lenten Tuesday

It's so early
the sky is still dark outside.
Cold air whispers across my skin through the open door
where Dad stands with his suitcase in one hand
        and his briefcase in the other,
while a car waits in the driveway, the engine humming low,
to take Dad to the airport.

He leans down to kiss a sleepy Kāia on the cheek,
then turns to Mama to give her a quick hug.
        He doesn't reach for me.
        He hasn't even looked at me
        since I thought
        I could fly.

"I'll call you from Spokane,"
he promises Mama,

making my hollow chest swell
with a tidal wave
of grief so great
it practically
knocks me
off
my
feet
roaring
Gina
Gina
Gina
Gina
Gina
Gina—

"Don't go."

All three
of them look
at me like I've finally
lost it.

"It's just four days, Aouli." Dad sighs,
like I am the cold air picking up,
like I am the breeze turned wind,

like I am pressing on his lungs,
making it hard to breathe.
"Be good, both of you."
But he's only
looking
at me.

My father,
the judge

of Pierce County Superior Court
of the innocent and the guilty
of this house
of my mother
of my sister
of my every waking move

of everyone
but himself.

Mama dances
when she cooks
dinner tonight
to Local music
blasting,
she sways
and spins
around
the kitchen, calling,
"Come on, Aouli girl!"
She swings her head
back
and forth.
"Sing it!"
And so,
I sing
the words I know
by heart
louder and
louder and
louder—

until Kāia yells
at us to stop,
but still
we keep singing
and soon
even she
starts to hum
along.

February 27

Lenten Friday

Our house
isn't a big house
or a fancy house
or a house people pass

and say, "Look at *that* one."

Our house
isn't a happy house
or a cool house
or a house full of laughter
or a house people walk into

and say, "I want to live *here*."

But when Dad is gone,
and I am free
to spend my evenings

with my feet up on the old coffee table,
the one handed down from Tūtū,
my grandmother,

listening to Mama laugh on the phone
with a friend back home in Kona,

watching Kāia flit around, long hair
pulled up in a floppy bun, talking out loud

to herself because she's not trying to
keep herself quiet,

our house
starts to feel
like a home.

February 28

Lenten Saturday

Dad's flight lands late tonight,
and I know I asked him to stay before he left,
and I know I gave him a chance to prove me wrong
about him,
about Gina Gina Gina Gina Gina Gina,
but he made his choice,
and the thought of his return makes my stomach rumble.

Because once he's back, there will be
no more
dancing
or singing
in the kitchen.

When we arrive at Aunty ʻEhu's house,
my little cousins run to greet me,
reaching their hands up and begging me to let them fly.

I show them the brace around my ankle
so they can see the truth,

    that none of us have wings.

It was all just playing pretend.

It's still too cold
to go outside,
so everyone stays warm

next to the fireplace,
gossiping in the kitchen,
laughing around the dining table,
gushing over my baby cousin,
fussing over the food,
all
together
beneath
one
roof.

I'm eating dessert.
Aunty 'Ehu's chocolate butter mochi.
Like brownies but way better.
And of course my mouth is full,
and my teeth are covered in chocolate,
when the front door opens and—

Nalu.

He's here.
Here here.
And I should have known he would be.

Of course he would. It's Aunty 'Ehu's house.

The center of the universe.

But still it's like an article out of a tabloid.
Spotted: Beyoncé Pumping Gas
She's Just Like You!
And the photo is so clearly fake
because there's no way Beyoncé pumps her own gas.

Just like there's no way Nalu could be standing
here in this house that raised me.

"Aouli, come. We should greet our guests."
Just like that Aunty 'Ehu is dragging me
up by my elbow, and I'm furiously
trying to scrub my teeth clean
with my tongue to get rid
of any evidence
that
I
eat

because she's taking me
to meet *Beyoncé*.

Only it's Nalu,

which
feels
so
much
more
stressful.

Nalu ducks into the house,
ukulele in hand, behind a broad-shouldered man
with a shiny bald head and a bright, familiar smile.

His dad, I think.

Stuck to Nalu's side is a little girl with a shy look in her eyes and black hair cascading down her back in two long braids.

They share the same wide nose
and round eyes.

Hers a warm brown, his full of stars.

All three of them make their way through the living room
the only way you can at a party full of Hawaiians.

Very, very slowly,

with hugs and strong slaps on the back,
with kisses on the cheek
and *how are you*s for everyone.

As they get closer, I try to make myself small
by tucking myself behind Aunty ʻEhu's slight frame,
hoping that maybe Nalu won't see me.

Aunty ʻEhu clicks her tongue.
"What are you doing?"

"Nothing—"

"Aouli?"

I wince.

"You two already met?" Aunty 'Ehu's fingers circle
tight around my wrist to yank me forward.

Nalu watches me expectantly, though not unkindly,
from beneath the edge of a beanie pulled low
over his waves.

I offer a close-lipped smile,
afraid that there are still bits of butter mochi
in my teeth. "Oh, hey, Nalu."

He returns with a grin.

And I swear the ache at my center starts to dull.

"This is my sister, Keala."
Nalu nudges the girl at his side. "Don't be shy."

Keala glares at him.

"Nice to meet you." I smile, so she knows I understand
exactly how annoying older siblings can be.

"Hi," she says quietly.

Aunty 'Ehu extends her hand toward Keala.
"Come with Aunty, let's go find the other keiki.
I think they're playing upstairs."

Keala looks at Nalu, silently asking for permission.
When he nods, she places her tiny hand in Aunty 'Ehu's
open palm.

"And, Aouli, why don't you show Nalu where the food is so he can make one plate?" Aunty 'Ehu jerks her chin toward the kitchen.

I open my mouth, hoping some excuse to go with them instead will just happen to fall out—

but Aunty 'Ehu doesn't even give me a chance
to come up with something
before she's whisking Keala away,

leaving Nalu and me
alone.

"Well, here it is."
I hold my arms out, presenting the spread
of food cluttering the kitchen counter.

Nalu reaches for a plate.
"Thanks for keeping me company."

He smiles, and my legs turn to jelly
in an instant.

Can he *stop* that?

"Yeah," I manage to squeak out. "I mean, sure.

Uh,

for

sure."

Pull

it

together,

Aouli!

"Oh, hell yeah," Nalu mutters to himself.

My eyebrows shoot up as he stills.
He even looks a little embarrassed?

I bite the inside of my cheek to keep myself
from smiling.

"What was that?" I pretend I didn't hear him.

He laughs at himself a little bit.
"Nothing, I—I just love chocolate butter mochi."

"Me too!"

And while my words come out way too loud,
he doesn't seem to notice
or care.

"Want me to grab you one?"

"No, it's okay." I shake my head.
"I already had a piece."

He shrugs. "So?"
He takes the plastic tongs,
plops another piece on a napkin,
and holds it out to me. "There should be no limits on joy."

I consider the mochi before taking it.
"So young, yet so wise?"

He laughs, and I'm sure my legs are one stray smile away
from disintegrating completely.

After a few more pieces of butter mochi,
Nalu and I end up side by side on the stairs,
and I'm painfully aware of the few inches
of space   between us.

I can hear all the little kids playing upstairs,
squealing without a single worry in the world.

It's one of the best parts of Aunty 'Ehu's house—

no one ever tells you to quiet down.

"Hey, um, I just wanted to say . . ." I trail off, trying to focus on the lines etched in my palms
instead of worrying about putting my foot in my mouth again.
"I'm sorry about your mom. I didn't know—"

"It's fine. Really." Nalu props his elbows on the step behind him.
He stares forward,
and I wonder what memories are coming to mind.
"There was no way you could have known."

"Still, it's probably hard."

"Yeah."

A few quiet moments pass between us, but for some reason this silence doesn't feel so bad.

"She was an artist." He looks at me, returning to the present.

"A really good one, apparently." I glance at the ukulele resting across his lap.

"Yeah." He smiles, but his eyes are sad. "She was."

One last conversation before it's time to go home.

Me: Are you mad your dad made you guys move?

Him: I was at first.

Him: I miss my friends.

Him: And surfing.

Me: Why did you have to move?

Him: Dad got a new job, but . . .

Me: What?

Him: Honestly?

Me: Of course.

Him: I think he just couldn't live there anymore without Mom.

Me: Ah.

Him: But now that we're here, it's not so bad.

March 6

Lenten Friday

I only get to go
on the youth group retreat
because Dad is naive
enough
to think
nothing bad ever happens
at church camp.

"Sneaking out is easy,"
Tia insisted at dinner. "But if you don't want to go,
you don't have to go."

And I didn't like the way she said that,
looking right at me, her voice barely sweet enough
to hide the challenge in her words.

So despite the nerves
grumbling in my stomach,

despite the threat
of what my father would do if I got caught,

I wait in the dark now
while the rest of my cabin sleeps,
eyes wide open, lying still as Sunday morning
in my bunk,

until I can summon the courage to

slip
out

the back
door—

I might not have wings,
but I refuse to stay stuck in this cage.

I run as fast as I can, ignoring
the pain radiating from my ankle,
the fear trailing in my tracks,
the ache in my chest that hasn't ebbed
since I found out about
Gina Gina Gina Gina Gina,

until I see Taylor and Tia waving me down
from where they've been waiting, crouched behind
the chapel building.

Tia stands. "Finally. We've been waiting for like
thirty minutes."

Taylor throws her arms around my neck and squeals
in my ear. "I can't believe
you actually
went through with it!"

But I can.
I can believe it.
I may have never tasted this
f r e e d o m

this sharp air,
this vast sky,
this night that promises
to keep all my secrets,

but that doesn't mean I haven't ever longed for it.

Finally I am free
to abandon
giggles
and whispering
and longing,

for singing and
squealing and
howling wild things
at the moon,

and to finally let
my longing
turn to
hunger.

We run until we reach the lake,
where I pause to marvel at the water,
at how smooth it is
and the way its glassy surface reflects the moon.

The forest around us is quiet.
There's no wind to unsettle the trees.
The air is cold, but I like the chill kissing my skin;
the buzzing in my blood is enough
to keep me warm.

For the first time
since I thought I could fly,

I feel alive.

The three of us
walk huddled together, following
the lake's rocky shore until the cabins
are so small in the distance I can fit
their faint silhouettes within an inch
          of space between
my thumb   and pointer finger.

After rounding a bend, I can finally see
our destination.

A fire, glowing orange against
the night to light
our way.

Taylor promised me it wouldn't be weird
to show up at an Apostles-only hangout,

but

it *is* weird.

They're *all* here.

I surprise myself though,
when my eyes don't search immediately
for Damien among them but

find Nalu instead—

I should have figured
it wouldn't be long
until they swooped in
and claimed him as their own.

Nalu holds court by the fire,
lounging against a rotting log,
his hands moving like magic
in sync with a story he's telling
that has everyone around him
leaning in close.

Firelight dances across his face,
and while I'm too far away
to make out every word,
I
too
am
entranced.

Tia

melds with the rest of the Apostles
into oneamorphousblob.

Are they like this at school, too?
So symbiotically linked.

Taylor doesn't skip a beat
before ditching me
to become

onewiththeblob,

making it painfully apparent
she's spent more time with the Apostles
during my grounding

than she's let on.

Tia runs straight to Nalu, knocking him over with a big hug.
It shouldn't come as a shock that Tia is into Nalu.
I mean, *look* at him.
I mean, look at *her*.

Tia is that classic-perfect-model type of pretty.
She is slender, tall (but not too tall), with big doe eyes
and a sweet voice that can make a boy unravel right on the spot.

Nalu and Tia make sense together!

They
totally
totally
totally
totally

do.

So why is it when Nalu smiles up at her, saying something
that makes her laugh, the bell-like sound grates like a screech?

So why am I suddenly so desperate for a way to block
it all out?

If I know they make so much sense together,
if I know I'm supposed to be shooting my shot with Damien,
if I know *I don't really know* this star-eyed boy,

why is it taking all my willpower to keep myself
from plugging my ears and screaming *la la la la la?*

I have to force myself
to look away, but when
I do? I realize
that
there
are
no
more
open
seats
around the fire,
and that I have been left
to stand outside
theblob,

that I've been left

alone.

The idea of leaving
starts to sound better the longer I stand here
looking like a total and complete idiot.

I could easily disappear back into the shadows
and let the night swallow me whole.

I could trudge back to my cabin and sleep off
the embarrassment of letting myself be dragged
all
the
way
out
here,

only to be ignored.

I take one step back.
    Taylor hasn't looked for me once.
    Not once.

I take another step back.
    Tia sits so close to Nalu
    she's practically in his lap,
    and he doesn't seem bothered one bit.

I take one more step.

Nalu hasn't even noticed me.

I start to turn away—

"Hey, Lily! Come over here!"

Did . . . ?

Huh?

Derek Miller, as in *Derek* Miller—

as in the third Miller brother in the D. Miller clan,
as in Damien Miller's older brother,
as in *the* Derek Miller, the object of
all my sister's desires—

just called
me (*me*)
over.

Derek waves me toward him as he makes space
for me to sit beside him, but I'm frozen
where I stand because I had no idea

Derek Miller even knew my name?

I don't know what to do.
I look at Taylor, then Tia, and finally
Nalu—

Oh, screw it.

I walk over and take the seat
beside Derek, hoping the shock isn't showing
so plainly on my face.
I try to seem cool,
collected,
and not at all rocked
to my very core.

"Hey." Derek smiles at me, and I realize
I've never been close enough to him
to notice how white his teeth are.

Like so white there's no way
he doesn't do those whitening strip things
that my dentist says are bad for enamel.

"Hi."

"Cold?" he asks.

I shrug. "Kind of." But I'm not.
I'm not.
I'm not.

"Here." He sheds his jacket
and throws it over my shoulders,

making it very clear
that Derek Miller is well-practiced
in keeping girls warm.

Like a note
out of key,
it's painfully obvious
that I don't belong here.

I look around.

What the hell
am I supposed to do
now—

a set of star eyes finds
mine.

Nalu.

Hey, he mouths.

Hey, I mouth back,
and only then do I start
to relax.

"Fuck, bro!"
Damien snatches his hand back from the fire.
Oh, what is the asinine game he and August are playing,
you ask?

No. Clue.

But I have gathered it involves holding your fingers over the flames
and swearing until you can't hold them there any longer.

My lips pinch.

Damien doubles over, cackling like the *pop pop pop* of the fire.

Derek rolls his eyes and mutters something under his breath.
He seems about as amused by his brother as I am,

and I can see why my sister writes *Kāia Miller* in her journal
over and over and over—

my sister.

Guilt charges through me,
and her name is Kāia.

What would she say if she saw me now
wearing Derek's jacket and sharing knowing looks with him
as Damien thrusts his hand into the flames again?
And is it just me or is Damien kind of . . . annoying?

There's a flask going around the circle.
When Derek offers it to me, I take a cautious pull
and pretend it doesn't burn
on
the
way
down.

The only alcohol I've ever had is the single sip
of sweet, blessed wine we get at church every Sunday—
whatever this is, it's not sweet,
and it's certainly not blessed.

I try to hand it back, but Derek nudges the flask toward me.
"It's fine, have more." He smiles at me,
like he's doing me a favor.

I brave a few more gulps and it's not long until
my head starts to feel fizzy.

And the drunker I get, the easier it is
to tell myself that Kāia's feelings don't matter.

It's not like I'm doing anything wrong.
It's not like she would have come along if I'd asked.
She would have told on us.
She would have kept me at the cabin.

This is what I tell myself.

This is what I believe, basking in the unexpected warmth of Derek's undivided attention.

Derek Miller
is handsome
like a cartoon prince
is handsome.
Not a fair hair
out of place.
Clear blue eyes.
Tall and broad-chested.
All he's missing
is a damsel in distress
looking for someone
to save her.

Derek talks to me
and only me
all   night   long.

He whispers to me, so only I
can hear him,

and people are starting to notice.

Tia. Taylor. I even catch Damien staring.
Damien, who has barely paid me a minute of attention
in the six years I've been in love with him.

Though maybe it isn't—
maybe it *never* was—

love.

Nalu is the only person
who doesn't seem to give a shit
about whatever alternate reality
I've found myself in.

He plucks at his ukulele—

like a limb,
it goes with him everywhere—

his nimble fingers moving easily
between strings.

As his strumming takes shape,
I recognize the tune immediately.

And right when I am sure
he can't surprise me more,

he
starts
to
sing.

Nalu doesn't have the perfect voice,
but it's striking nonetheless.

Derek and I continue to catch side looks and stares,
but my eyes remain fixed on this boy
who has a talent

for catching me off guard in the most

unexpected
ways.

Memory
Eight Years Ago
It's summertime in Hawai'i,

and I'm flying
somewhere between

the blue sky above

and the blue sea below.

Life feels so simple
rolling down Queen Ka'ahumanu Highway,
a road that cuts straight across
the land for miles.

Papa—my grandfather—drives us
in his old red truck with the rusted hood
from years of exposure to the sun and ocean air.
Kāia and I are right on the edge of being too big
to squish in next to him on the bench seat,
our skin coated in sweat and sand
from a long day at the beach.
Dad's in the back by himself,
tucked in tight with our salt-beaten body boards.

"Ho! Kāia, girl. Get the volume fo' me."
Papa slaps the dash with his palm.

Kāia cranks the dial to the right,
filling the truck with the sweet sounds of HAPA
as Papa's and Dad's voices soar with the song.

Dad squeezes my shoulder. "Let's hear it, Aouli!"

So I hang my arm out the window
to let the wind ribbon between my fingers
as my own voice

rises

to join

with

theirs.

I forget.

I forget that I am not in Kona.

I forget that Papa is gone.

I forget that Dad is probably bent over his computer back in Hawk Valley.

I forget that Kāia is still fast asleep in our cabin.

I forget that *nothing* is simple.

I forget that I am not flying in the wind.

I forget,

and that's when I let myself

sing.

Nalu's fingers freeze,
causing a skip in the song
and jolting me back to reality.

His eyes find mine
immediately,
and

then

the

world

falls

quiet.

Star eyes
pierce into mine,
and in them

I see
both the beginning

and the end
of a thousand skies.

An e x p a n s e of blue.

When the world rushes back,
I remember the rocks digging into my backside.
I remember the heat from the fire tickling my skin.
I remember everyone's eyes on me.
I remember Derek's jacket heavy on my shoulders.
I remember Nalu's dancing fingers.
I remember Dad.
I remember Kāia.
I remember Gina Gina Gina Gina Gina.
I remember

I

am

not

the

sky.

A conversation turned interrogation.

Me: Why are you staring at me?
Derek: You can sing?
Me: Everyone can sing.
Me: If they want to, that is.
Derek: How did you know that song?
Me: It was my grandfather's favorite song.
Derek: What kind of language was that, anyways?
Me: Hawaiian.
Derek: You speak Hawaiian?
Me: Not really.
Derek: Then how did you know it?
Me: I just know the lyrics.
Derek: Are you, like, from there?
Me: From where?
Derek: Hawai'i.

But he pronounces it like Ha-WHY.

Which is incorrect.

And annoying as shit.

Me: No.
Me: *I'm* Hawaiian.
Derek: Oh. Ha.
Me: What?
Derek: I mean, I just didn't know.
Derek: It's not like you look like it.

I don't look like it?

My hair is dark like the starless sky untouched by city lights.
My eyes are green like the speckled backs of slithering mo'o.
My jaw is strong like the rounded edge of a pōhaku pounding poi.
My skin is smooth like pāhoehoe from a hundreds-of-years-old flow.
My hips are full like the moon rising over Mauna Kea.
My feet are tough like 'opihi stuck to jagged cliffsides.

I don't look like it?

I am a descendant of the Earth Grandmother.
Of the Sky Father.
Of the Star Mother.
Of the Kānaka Maoli. The people.
My people.
I am—

Derek is laughing.

And the others,
the ones who've been watching,
they start laughing, too.
But I don't get the joke.
That is, until I realize
that
the
joke
is
me.

I am a joke.

I am trapped *I am trapped*
in a hall of mirrors *in a hall of mirrors*

everywhere *everywhere*
I *I*
turn *turn*

wide *wide* open *open* mouths *mouths*

laugh *laugh* laugh *laugh* laugh *laugh*
at me *at me*

there is no way out *there is no way out*
there is no way out *there is no way out*
there is no way out of this fun house *there is no way out of this fun house*

so I cower *so I cower*

like the coward *like the coward*

I am. *I am.*

The sound
of a thousand
mirrors

sha tter ing

into a

tho usa nd pie ces

silences

the laughter.

And when I find
the courage to finally look up,
buried somewhere deep
in my bones,
I see two risen stars
to
light
a
path
to
guide
me
through
this
shattered
house and back into the night.

"What's a Hawaiian supposed to look like, Miller?"
A familiar rhythm, like the beat of an ipu,
picks up in Nalu's voice,
and it dawns on me that Nalu
has been softening his accent.

Derek is still laughing,
like we're still in the fun house.

"Is there a problem?"

My cheeks flame.

Nalu's eyes flick to me.

I shake my head.

No.

And that small gesture is enough to push the shadows
from Nalu's face and to draw back his carefree grin,
though there's an edge to it now
that wasn't there before.
He sets his ukulele aside.
There will be no more music tonight.

"Never mind, bro."

And I can no longer hear
the beat of the ipu.

Someone suggests we head back.
The fire is extinguished.
The blankets are gathered.
People start to head toward the cabins.

Taylor walks ahead,
arm in arm with Tia,
and I don't have it in me to be upset
that my best friend has traded me in.

That my best friend didn't do anything
to help me out of the fun house.

I have   nothing
left
to give
this night.

Someone grabs me
by my waist,
startling me so bad it feels like
                              lightning
                         striking
          me right through
                    the hole
                         in my
                              chest.

Derek doesn't apologize for scaring me,
for grabbing me without asking.
Which makes me think that girls
don't usually complain when Derek Miller
touches them.

Or if they do,
he doesn't listen.

"I liked talking to you tonight." His breath reeks.

What would Kāia say,

if she knew her godly boy drank alcohol and grabbed girls
just because he could?

What would she say if she knew he trapped me in his fun house
because I was not,
because I am not,
what he wanted me to be?

Derek Miller might look like a prince,
but I have no interest
in being his
damsel.

I shrug him off,
hoping it seems like I'm just removing his jacket,
because that feels safer
than actually
telling
him
no.

"Hold on to it," he insists.
"That way I can keep you warm tonight."

The implication sets off alarms in my head
screaming screaming screaming at me.

Run!

Go!

Get out of here!

But I am trapped I am trapped I am trapped
by my own fear, frozen
in place, as he presses
a cold
damp
kiss
on
my
mouth.

I have dreamed
a hundred different daydreams
of my first kiss.
How it would feel.
Where it would be.
Who it would be with.
But *that* was not my dream.
        It was a nightmare.

It was just a kiss.
A kiss I didn't even want.
A kiss I didn't even initiate.

So why does it feel
like I've done something
terribly
terribly
wrong?

There's a smirk brewing on Derek's face
as his gaze shifts from me to someone else
behind me.

He chuckles. "Night, *bro*."

Then he slinks off into the night.

When he's gone,
I turn
to see
Nalu
staring back at me
without a trace of starlight flickering in his eyes.

A truly terrible conversation.
Me: What?
Nalu: Nothing.
Me: You look like you have something to say, so say it.
Nalu: That guy is an ass. Are you really into him like that?
Me:
Me: Why do you even care?
Nalu: I don't care.
Me: It seems like you do.
Nalu: It's just—
Me: What?
Nalu: Earlier—

Me: What?

Nalu: At the fire.

Me: *What?* Spit it out, Jesus Christ—

Nalu: You did nothing! You just took his shit! Like what was *that* about?

Me: What was I supposed to do?

Nalu: Stand up for yourself! I shouldn't have had to—

Me: I didn't ask you for anything. If it was that much trouble to defend me—

Nalu: I wouldn't have had to defend you if you'd defended yourself!

Me: Why does it matter to you? You don't even know me.

Nalu:

Me: Forget it. I'm going to go. I'm exhausted.

Nalu: Aouli, wait—

Me: And no.

Me: I'm not into Derek like that.

Dream

Rain

pummels the earth

with so much force

it sounds like the sky is screaming,

it looks like the ground is steaming,

and the crow
the poor, lonely crow

searches
searches
searches   for a way out
                            of the storm.

March 7

Lenten Saturday

"You know the rules, Miss Lily."
Sister Tammy smiles down at me, and I wonder
if she's like this because she gets some sick satisfaction
from making our lives   a living   *hell.*

Yes.

I know the rules.

Breakfast begins promptly
at 7:00 a.m., and if you're late,

prepare to take the punishment in full.

That means song
and dance.

I wouldn't have been late
if I hadn't been up most of the night
and into the early morning,

tossing and turning,

            in and out of strange dreams,

my thoughts tumbling,

            just trying to forget about

Derek Miller,
the fun house,
the kiss,
Nalu and our fight beside the lake.

"Chop-chop!" Sister Tammy flashes a gummy smile
at me. "Get your tush up to the front of the room.
We don't have all day."

I look at Taylor, squeezed between Tia and Katie
at a long table with the rest of the Apostles.
            Good luck, she mouths.

I look at Kāia—
            why did I look at Kāia?

She looks even giddier than Sister Tammy.
                                                Bitch!

Sister Tammy holds out a hand,
directing me toward the breakfast buffet,
the backdrop to my performance.

My feet drag the entire way,
dreading dreading dreading dreading—

"I'll do that dance with Aouli."

Everyone's heads swivel
in unison to look
at the only person in this room
who has ever
called me

Aouli.

(Besides my giddy, bitchy sister.)

"Thank you, Nalu,"
Sister Tammy says, and I hate I hate I hate I hate I *hate*
the way she says his name,
            like her nostrils are stuffed with tissue.
"That's sweet," she says. "But you were on time."
She directs her smile back at me.
"Lily was not—"

But Nalu is gone, marching right out of the dining hall,
leaving all of us to stare speechless after him
as the screen door
slap   *slap*   *slaps* closed behind him.

After
the
longest
ten
seconds
ever,

Nalu comes back, throwing open the door.
"Looks like I'm late now, too."

Without a glance at Sister Tammy,
he saunters past her
to stand
right next to   me.

Feeling frantic, I start to whisper,
"You don't have to—"

But he cuts me off
with the back of his hand brushing
up against the back of mine, as if to say,

> Don't worry,
> you're not alone;
> I won't let them trap you in that fun house
> ever again.

Then he begins to sing
and dance.

To be sung to the tune of "I'm a Little Teapot"

I'm a little worried
for my heart.
The way it sings!
The way it howls!
When I am around him
my insides
shout!

Shit! I like him.
Fuck! What now?

Everyone—
everyone except Sister Tammy—
cheers us on

as Nalu and I perform,

as we become increasingly more ridiculous
with each repetition of the song,

as we sing-scream so loud my throat is stiff and scratchy
by the time Sister Tammy finally has enough.

"Okay!" She waves her hands over her head.
"You've made your point!"

Caught up in the moment, I intertwine my fingers with Nalu's,
throwing our hands up into the air before bowing
so deeply the ends of my braids brush the floor.

When we come back up, everyone is
banging their fists against the tables,
clapping their hands,
chanting our names,

and it turns out there's nothing that brings a youth group
of divided factions together
like a common enemy.

It's not until the camp cook
barges out of the kitchen to shout,
"If you want to eat, shut your yaps!"
that everyone finally settles down and the room returns
to a normal volume.

Now, however, there is a renewed sense of justice
and the swelling pride of a small victory
buzzing just beneath
the chatter.

I look at Nalu. "Thanks."

He looks at me. "I'm sorry."

"Why are you sorry?"

"For last night . . ." He looks down,

and my eyes follow to that place where our hands are still
twined together—

I let go.

I let go because
I am sure,

I am sure that if he were to pull away first,
I would never recover, I would never survive knowing

what it feels like to be left
by him.

Still buzzing after breakfast,
I run straight back to my cabin
for Derek's jacket.

When I find him at the basketball court,
playing a game with Damien and Landon,
    I can feel Kāia's eyes on me,
    watching me from the nearby picnic table
    she's at with Julie.

Derek takes a shot, the ball ricocheting off the rim.

Landon holds his fist to his mouth. "Ohhhhhhh!"
    "Weak, dude!" Damien taunts his brother.
Derek shoves him in the back, trying to play it off
like he's not actually really mad—

    but I know that look, I live with that look,

    I am intimately familiar
    with the terrifying truth
    of
    that
    look.

I'm not normally a patient person,
but this is something
I can wait for at the edge of the court

until Derek finally notices me.

I toss him his jacket.

He reaches to catch it in midair.

"You can keep it another night, you know."
He flashes that too-white smile at me,
and suddenly I feel sick.

Derek Miller is not the prince.

He's the villain.

I do my best to stand tall. "Thanks, but I didn't need it.
I was plenty warm on my own."

Damien's and Landon's eyebrows shoot up.

I don't know what Derek says,
if he says anything at all.

I'm already gone.

Kāia marches after me
to corner me outside our cabin.
"What the fuck was that!"

I press the back of my hand to her forehead.
My sister *never* swears. "Are you unwell?"

She slaps my hand away.

"*Ow.*" I cradle my hand to my chest.

A shadow passes over her face.
If looks could kill
                                I'd be dead in the grass.

"What just happened?" she grinds out.

I consider telling her. It's all right there
at the press of my lips,
threatening
to spill
          out
                    between   us.

But I know that with the truth
about Derek, everything
would come.

Dad.
Gina.
Gina.
Gina.
Gina.
Gina.

And now,

Derek.
Derek.
Derek.
Derek—

I keep my mouth shut and swallow
each name back down to sour
            in my stomach.

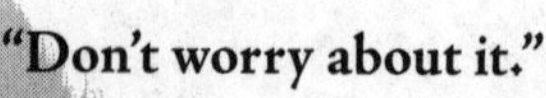

"Don't worry about it."

Kāia shrinks.

"But it—it's Derek, Aouli."

Her voice is suddenly small and meek,
and that makes me angry.

I hate the way she says his name.

Like it's an explanation.
Like he's that powerful.

"What does that even mean, Kāia?
It's not like you're his girlfriend.
I can talk to Derek if I want;
just because you're obsessed with him
doesn't mean you have ownership over him."

Her lips part in surprise.

I craft each word
to sting,
to hurt,
to keep her an arm's length away,

so that she finally
lets me
go.

Guilt

looms over me

like late-morning cloud cover

as I watch my sister leave,

and I wonder if there will ever come the day when

I will be brave enough

to

not

push

her

away.

March 8

Third Sunday of Lent

I wake up early, before everyone else,
thinking about

everything
about Dad
about Gina
about Derek
about Nalu

about Kāia.

So I wrap my blanket around my shoulders,
tuck my song journal under my arm,
tiptoe past my sister's bunk,
and walk out to the lake
to sit on the shore
and sing
something
to the waking sun.

something unfinished
I have this dream that I can fly
that I have wings to touch the sky
~~maybe someday~~ one day
I will finally soar high

"What are you writing?"

I slam my notebook closed, pinching my finger
in the process. "*Ow.* Jesus Chr—"

"Shit, I'm sorry!" Nalu backs away quickly.
"I didn't mean to sneak up on you like that. I couldn't sleep
and I saw you were out here and—" He cuts himself off
with a sigh.
"I can go—"

"Don't." The word erupts out of me.
Too harsh.
Too loud.
Too *frantic.*

But my worry is quickly put to rest
when he takes a seat in the grass next to me,
resting his ukulele in his lap.

"Well, if you really don't want me to go." He grins at me,
in a way that sets my skin on fire.
He's still in his pajamas,
flannel pants and a University of Hawai'i hoodie
that's frayed at all the edges.
"So," he begins softly, as if not to startle me again.
"What are you writing?"

I burrow deeper into my blanket, taking my journal with me.
"It's nothing. I mean, not *nothing.* Lyrics. Well, pieces of lyrics."

I cringe.
Why did I have to say that?

"You're a songwriter." His grin widens.

"Barely. I can't even play an instrument. They're just . . ." I cradle my journal closer into my chest. ". . . words."

"Some would say that's the most important part."

I roll my eyes. "And many would say the most important part of a song is the *music*."

"Eh." He picks up his ukulele, his fingers landing gracefully on the frets as he strums a single, bright chord.

"If you really need music,
I can play for you."

I swallow, oddly touched, yet desperate not to show it. "Are you willing to audition?"

"Whatevah." He shoves my shoulder playfully with his own, sending every fiber of my being into

an

all-out

frenzy.

A conversation I'll replay in my head over and over and over.

Nalu: This reminds me, there's something I need to talk to you about.

Me: Oh God. What?

Nalu: When were you going to tell me you're a singer?

Me: . . . Never?

Nalu: Come on. Your voice is kick-ass.

Me: It's really not.

And when I say *it's really not* I don't mean *it really is.*
I mean *it's really* not.

Nalu: Ah, so you're like the brooding, tortured, humble type of artist?

Me: Shut *up*.

Nalu: But seriously, though, when do I get to hear you sing again?

Me: Ha. You're hilarious, you know that?

Nalu: Come on, Aouli.

Me: I don't sing in public.

Nalu: But last night—

Me: Will haunt me for the rest of my days. I don't sing in front of people.

Me: Not anymore.

Nalu: So you used to?

Me: I was in the church choir for like a *year*. But it was stupid and boring and—

Me: What?

Nalu: What?

Me: You're looking at me funny.

Nalu: No, I'm not.

Me: Yes, you—

Nalu: Can I read your song?

Nalu: The one you're writing?

Me: No.

Nalu: What if I ask nicely?

Me: Cute, but *no*.

Nalu: Well, what if you kept writing?

Nalu: I'll just sit here.

Nalu: I won't talk.

Me: Ah—

Nalu: And I won't peek.

Me: Promise?

Nalu: Promise.

Me: Fine.

Me: No staring *longingly* at me, either.

Nalu: Ha-ha. Very funny.

Memory

Three Years Ago

"Again." Dad won't let me go to sleep.

Not until I sing my solo for the Easter concert
without a single mistake.
Not until he's torn me apart note by note.
Not until I'm perfect.

I start to sing, but it hurts.
My throat is scratchy from hours of practice.
My legs are sore from standing for so long.

My heart aches from every time he makes me
do it again
again again again again.

"Please, Dad." Tears sting my skin
as they roll down my face.

Dad closes his eyes like he's praying. "Again."

The last night of every youth group retreat
always ends with Adoration.

It's basically an hour of your life
you can never get back,

standing on your knees,
holding your hands in prayer,
staring at a piece of bread

and pretending to be grateful for it.

When I find Taylor in the chapel,
there's no space around her for me to sit.

"Sorry, babe. I didn't know
if you wanted me to save you a seat."

"So you just didn't?"

And at least she has the decency
to look a little embarrassed.

"Whatever. It's fine." Scanning the pews,
I try to find an open seat.

There's one next to Kāia.

I could—?

But I don't,

because she's still angry at me,
because I pushed her too far away,
because I'm still scared
I'll tell her everything,

so I take a seat in the last pew
all by

myself.

"Can I sit with you?"
Nalu stands at the entrance to my pew,
waiting
for my answer.

"Sure" is all I say, but inside
I'm really saying,

Yes. Of course. Are you kidding me?

Please. SIT.

Don't you get it?

Do you not understand

how freaking hot you are
all
the
time?
And kind.
And nice.
And funny, too.

Yes, Nalu.
Of course you can sit next to me.

You can sit next to me
for an hour,

forever,
for as long as you want,

because I don't think I could ever tire
of how it feels
to
be
next
to
you.

The minutes
tick

tick

tick

tick

tick by slowly,

and it feels like this hour
will never
end,

so when my arms start to ache
from holding my hands up for so long,

I peek over my shoulder to make sure
Sister Tammy isn't looking
before   resting   my arms   at my sides.

And then,
out of the corner of my eye,
I watch Nalu's hand drop between us—

one

two

three—

his finger slips
around mine,
setting
me
off
like a firework.

Maybe
Adoration isn't so bad?

Sitting like this, with a knuckle's worth
of skin touching his,
I
could
worship
all
night.

March 9

Lenten Monday

Dad is talking to me again.
Which is good,
I guess.
I got my phone back, too,
and I'm finally allowed to hang out
in my room with the door closed.
But still, only home.
But still, only school.
But still, only church.
But still, only cages
that feel like
they're only
getting
smaller
and

s

m

a

l

l

e

r.

Texts

8:30 p.m.

?: Hey!

Me: Who's this?

?: Guess

Me: STRANGER DANGER

?: Ugh. You're no fun.

?: It's Nalu :)

9:21 p.m.

Me: Hiiiii. Sorry sorry.

Me: I was doing homework.

I was not.

I was freaking out.

Nalu: It's all good

Nalu: I got your number from your sister.

Nalu: I hope that's okay?

Me: You asked her?

Nalu: Yeah!

Me: And she didn't bite you?

Me: Aren't you lucky?

Nalu: I like to think so.

March 10

Lenten Tuesday

Twenty-four hours later,
I finally drum up enough nerve to ask Kāia,

"Why did you give Nalu my number?"

> I've gone over it a million times,
> trying to understand why,
> worried this is all just some sick prank.
> It
> doesn't
> make
> any
> sense
> especially after what I said to her.

It's just us two in the living room.
She's studying for a science test.
I'm procrastinating writing an essay.

"Because he asked," she mutters,
without looking up from her note cards.

"Kāia." I shut my laptop.

"Aouli." She mocks my tone.

"What gives?" I cross my arms.

She glances up at me blankly. "Care to elaborate?"

"A *boy* asking for my number is certainly
grounds for having me sent to a convent.
Why haven't you snitched yet?"

I expect her
to volley back,
to dig in,
to roll her eyes,
to brush me off,
anything but—

"Do you really think I am that coldhearted?"
She sets her note cards down, gathering her long legs
to her chest and curling back into the couch.
She looks so small coiled up like that.
She eats too little.
She worries too much.

Just like Mama.

My answer is automatic. "No, I don't."

"Liar." She picks up her note cards again
and starts flipping through.

I slowly reopen my laptop, watching her eyes
dart between formulas.

"Well. Thanks."

Her eyes still. "Sure. Just don't tell Dad, okay?"

I don't respond,
but I know
she knows
I won't.

After a few silent minutes,
Kāia murmurs, "I think he likes you."

"Who?" I ask, acting like I don't know.

"*Nalu,* you freak. Stop trying to be all coy.
You're bad at it."

"Oh." I sink deeper into the couch.
"You think so? I haven't really thought
about him
like that,
I mean."

Kāia shakes her head, the corner of her mouth
perking up. "Shut up and write your essay."

March 13

Lenten Friday

Nalu and I text
all day every day
this week.

I complain to him about Spanish class.
He tells me about how mean the St. Joseph's nuns are.
I grumble to him about the long lunch lines.
He counters that food is worth it.
I maintain that *this* food isn't.
He tells me about his history teacher, how she keeps trying
to show him pictures from her family's Hawai'i vacation.
I tell him about Taylor and Jake, how they got detention
for ditching third period to make out behind the gym.
He brags about how he gets to wear jeans to school on Thursdays.

I remind him that, at public school, you can wear jeans every day
if you want.
He sends me pictures of his tūtū's dog, Pepe.
I send him pictures of the doodles I draw in my math notebook.
He bothers me for a look at my song journal.
I distract him with actual songs I want him to listen to.
He responds with whole paragraphs of his thoughts.
And when I tell him it's late, that I need to go to bed,
he always tells me to sleep well, and that he will talk to
me
tomorrow.

I wake up
to Dad screaming
at Mama about
I don't know,
something,
nothing.
I try to block it out.
I try to bury my head in my pillow.
I try to pretend it's not happening.
But I can't.
I can't.
I can't.

I charge in

and throw myself between them

put my hands up

like I wish Mama would for me,

and I beg him to "Stop!"

But I am shoved aside.

"Just stop!"

But I am told to leave.

"Please stop!"

But I am forced to listen

to him scream all night, and now

it's

about

me.

Dear God,

What the hell
are you doing up there
watching
idly
as
we
burn?

Amen.

Dream

A crow's wings are set aflame

help!
help!
help!

she screams
but there is no one
so she plummets
in a blaze

March 14

Lenten Saturday

Texts

8:03 a.m.

Nalu: I have good news and bad news

Nalu: Which first?

Me: Good news pls

Nalu: Interesting . . .

Nalu: You definitely have bad news first vibes

Me: What's that supposed to mean????

Nalu: I wouldn't worry about it

Nalu: I got into Seattle U

Me: OMG. That's so exciting!!!!!!

Nalu: Thank u thank u

Me: Waitttttt. I thought you already decided to go to UH Manoa?

Nalu: Eh. I like to have my options open.

Nalu: Besides, Washington is growing on me.

Me: Hold on. What's the bad news???

Nalu: My dad is taking me and Keala into Seattle to celebrate.

Nalu: So I won't be at Aunty 'Ehu's today :(

Nalu: So you will have to try your best to survive without me

Me: Need I remind you I survived seventeen years without you?

Nalu: Oh just admit it.

Nalu: You're going to miss me.

I'm going to miss you.

Mama and Dad

go on this morning
like they always do.
Like nothing
happened,
like everything
is normal.

Which I guess it is.
For us.

Texts

11:36 a.m.

Nalu: I almost forgot to ask!

Nalu: Any good dreams last night?

Me: *Typing . . .*

Me:

Me: Nah

Me: Couldn't really sleep.

"You been quiet today, honey girl."
Aunty 'Ehu uses my shoulder to help herself
down into the seat next to mine. When she's settled,
she pats my cheek.

We're the only ones left at the dining table, and I can hear all the adults talking in the living room, Dad's voice rising above the rest.

He's talking about Kāia,
how she should be getting her acceptance letter
from Yale any day now.
(Rejection, of course, has never been entertained as an option.)

I shrug. "I'm just tired."

Aunty 'Ehu tuts. "Oh, you too young fo' be tired. Just wait until you become an old fut like me."

"You're not old."

"Good answer. Your mama trained you well." She chuckles for a few beats before it turns into a shallow cough.

"My point exactly."

I sit up, placing my hand on her back. "Can I get you water?"

But she just brushes me off. "No worry about me; I'm okay."

"You're stubborn," I mutter.

"It's hereditary," she counters,
wiping her mouth with the back of her hand.
"Now tell me, honey girl, what's wrong."

I don't know how to answer her question without telling her about Dad.

About Gina Gina Gina Gina.

About Derek.

So I ask her a question instead.

"Do you pray?"

She nods. "'Ae. Every day."

"And how do you know if God's actually listening
or not?"

"Oh, I don't pray to that guy. Too much on his plate,
don't know why he would ever pay attention to me."

"Who are you praying to, then?"

She sits back, with a little smile on her face, like I asked
exactly what she was hoping I would.

"I ka wā kahiko,
we did not worship
just one god, but hundreds,
maybe thousands. And they did not rule
only from the sky, but lived
all around us.

"Kāne as the dawn.
Kū as the canoe.
Lono as the wai.
Kanaloa as the he'e.
Pele as the crater.
Hi'iaka as the lehua.
Laka as the hula.
Poli'ahu as the snow.
Papahānaumoku as the earth.
Hāloanakalaukapalili as the kalo,
and on and on and on.

"Then there were
our 'aumakua, our ancestors, our protectors.
You remember ours, yeah?
'Alalā.
The crow.

"So, honey girl,
when I pray—
and I do so every day—
I pray to her. Because I don't know
if God got time for old futs like me.
But one thing I know for sure?
Our ancestors?
They are *always* with us."

Texts

6:00 p.m.

Taylor: Hey girl heyyyyyy

Me: She's alive?!?!?!

Taylor: Wdym??? Lol

Me: I haven't heard from you in like a week.

Me: And we have two classes together lol.

Taylor: Hehehe sorry I know I've been MIA

Taylor: BUT let me make it up to you

Taylor: Sleepover at my house tonight?

Taylor: Just you and meeeee babyyyyyyy

Me: My dad probably won't let me stay over.

Taylor: Ugh how much longer are you grounded for??

Me: Ends tomorrow.

Taylor: Okay so it's basically over?!

Me: Maybe I could still hang out for a little while? Just not sleep over?

Taylor: YES

Taylor: now get your ass over here!!!

After *a lot* of begging,
Dad finally agrees to let me go.
"Two hours, that's it.
Then I'm sending your sister to pick you up."

When I get to Taylor's house,
she fills me in on everything I've apparently missed
since the last time we talked.

Which was *when*, exactly?

I struggle to remember.

It's mostly
Jake stuff and
school stuff and
SAT prep stuff,
until—

"Oh, *also*!" Taylor flings herself back
on her bed next to me.

I turn onto my side to face her,
propping my head up on my elbow.

I missed this.

"You and Nalu are friends, right?"
The question throws me at first, but then
I'm *bursting*.

I've been dying to talk to her about Nalu.

It's weird that I haven't,
so much so
I almost feel
guilty
about it,
like I'm hiding something from her.

Normally she would have known everything
by now,

every smile,
every accidental brush of skin,
every conversation,
every text;
every mundane moment
would have already been
detailed,
dissected,
and analyzed—

but it's not like there's been much opportunity
to talk to her about   anything.
Between her sneaking off with Jake at school
            and never leaving Tia's side at church,

Taylor hasn't had much time lately

for me.

"Has he said anything to you about Tia at all?"

I blink.

"Tia?"

"Yeah? *Tia.* Lily?
God,
you've been so
spacey lately."

Taylor laughs,
but I don't get what's funny.

She watches me expectantly,
waiting for an answer to a question
I'm still struggling to understand.

"Why would Nalu talk to me
about Tia?"

Taylor sighs, like I should know this already.

"St. Joseph's Spring Fling is soon,
but he hasn't asked her yet."

I draw away. "Uh—"

"We thought since you two are like Hawai'i buds
or whatever, maybe he talked to you about it?
You know, bro to bro."

We?

Hawai'i buds?

Bro to bro?

Taylor whips out her phone, rocking up to a seat.

"Yeah, I mean, it's weird, right?" She won't stop talking.
"Tia needs to get over here; we need to game plan." And texting.
"You're cool with that, right?"

Is this what whiplash feels like?

"Wait—um—" I scratch behind my ear.
"Why is it weird he hasn't asked her yet?"

Taylor gapes at me. "You don't *know?*"
She lowers her voice
and leans in.
"They're
totally
hooking up."

Memory

Nine Years Ago

I'm eight years old, and I've climbed one of
the great maple trees in Aunty 'Ehu's backyard.

Even though Dad told me I couldn't.
Even though Kāia swore she would tell if I did.

So when Kāia keeps her promise, Dad yells
so loud it startles me off my branch.

I fall, tumbling to the earth. And when I hit the ground,
the impact smacks the air right out of me.

For several panicked moments,
I can't breathe.

But when I finally start breathing again, when I finally
manage to choke down a few gasps full of air—

that's when the real pain
starts.

That's how it feels
when Taylor tells me
about Tia and Nalu.

Like falling.
Like hitting the earth.
Like struggling to breathe.

Like pain.
Like pain.
Like pain.

March 15

Fourth Sunday of Lent

"It's time to begin prepping for Stations of the Cross!"
Sister Tammy claps her hands together.
"And I know you are *all* very excited, so let's get started!"

I bite back a groan. Today is going to suck.

Youth group is in the nave today,
and we're all seated in the first two rows of pews,
forced to watch Sister Tammy as she excitedly paces

back and forth
back and forth.

And despite trying my best to avoid Nalu at all costs—

"What's Stations of the Cross?" The sound of his voice
from behind me winds me up so tight,
I'm one more (perfectly fair) question out of him before I *snap.*

"It's this weird crucifixion play we do every Easter," Tia whispers.
"I'll probably be Mary this year."

Interesting.

Especially considering everyone knows it's guaranteed
that whoever plays Mary and Jesus will bang by Easter.
Unless they're already banging.
It's practically a youth group tradition.

Tia gasps and my fingers curl into fists.
"You would be a perfect Jesus. You *have* to volunteer."

Yep.

That'll do it.

Sister Tammy tells us to split up.
"If you want to do stage crew, sit on the left;
if you want to be an actor, sit on the right."

Tia is out of her seat in a flash, strutting around the pews
and to the right like she's on her way to collect a freaking Oscar.

"Hey, you coming?" Nalu's hand on my shoulder
surprises me at first,
then turns me to stone.

I shrug away. "I'm more of a stage crew kind of girl."

He swings around from the second pew.
"Smart. Talented singer and talented actor is too killer of a combo.
Can't let you become too powerful, can we?"

I slide out and around him, careful
not to touch him.

His brows crease. "Aouli?"

But I'm already walking away.

I don't make it very far though
when I realize Taylor,
who has always done stage crew with me,
isn't
behind me.

Instead, she's making a beeline
across the chapel
to join *Tia*.

I get her attention.
What the hell? I mouth, looking at her like
excuse me,
what are you doing?
We always do stage crew together.

And she just stares back, like
it's fine,
don't be dramatic,
we don't always have to do everything together.

But I know what it really means
is that she doesn't *want* to do this together,
not anymore.

"Seems like a few people want the same roles,"
Sister Tammy announces. "I'll make the final decision
and send out the cast list tomorrow."

I watch Tia and Taylor bend their heads together,
I watch them whisper back and forth,
I watch the way their shoulders shake as they giggle
over an inside joke I'll never understand.

Sister Tammy reminds us. "Rehearsals are Wednesday evenings
and Sundays after church at our usual time! Don't forget!"

And as soon as we're dismissed, I'm the first one
to make it to the door—

I can't fucking *breathe* in here.

Texts

7:41 p.m.

Nalu: Hey, are you okay?

Nalu: You seemed kind of off today at church.

11:55 p.m.

Nalu: Aouli?

March 16

Lenten Monday

Email

From: holywarrior1@yahoo.com

To: lily.smith@gmail.com

Subject: Stations of the Cross Cast List

Stage Crew

Lily (Aouli), August, Julie W., Brady, Jessie

Narrators

Lola, Luke

Weeping Women

Tia, Taylor, Julie S., Abby, Katie

Criminals

Nalu, Landon

Simon of Cyrene

Garrett

Pontius Pilate

Damien

Mary, Mother of Christ

Kāia

Jesus Christ

Derek

May God Bless You!

Tammy

Tamara Vasquez
Director of Youth and Teen Programming
St. Peter's Church

At the end of the email, I feel
relief,
          then guilt,
                    and finally, fear.

Not Kāia. Not with *him*.

I should tell her.
I should warn her.

But I don't.
I don't.
I don't.
I don't.

And I don't know why.

March 17

Lenten Tuesday

The lights are too bright
in the exam room at the doctor's.

"You'll still have to wear the brace
during any strenuous physical activity
for the next twelve weeks,
but other than that,
you're free!"

No,
Doctor,   I'm not.

"And next time you want to go
from the second floor to the first,
promise me you will just take the stairs?
Unless you plan on sprouting wings
anytime soon?"

No,
Doctor,   I don't.

The lights in here are too bright,
and the pain is much too loud.

March 18

Lenten Wednesday

The doors to the nave are locked
and Sister Tammy is late to the first rehearsal,
so I'm waiting in the narthex with Taylor
        doing my best to pretend to care
        while she vents to me about Jake.

"He
is
pissing
me
off."

Taylor's voice echoes throughout the narthex,
drawing sideways looks from some of the others.

I'd picked my spot—
tucked away in the corner on the floor
with my back up against one of the stone pillars—
hoping to have some quiet time (alone)
to work on the song I started at camp.
          Then Taylor showed up.
          Without a *hey* or a *how are you,*
          she hip-checked me to the side,
          claimed half of my spot as her own,
          and started yelling about her dumb boyfriend.

"What did Jake do?" I ask, but my heart's not in it.

Not that Taylor notices.

"He only wants to play video games
when I go over to his house.
It's annoying."

"Yeah." I'm not even looking at her.
"That's annoying." I'm staring at my journal.

"That's it?"

"What do you mean?" I mutter, tapping my pen,
ink freckling the page.

She frowns. "You're not being helpful. Like at all."

I close my journal with a snap.
Even if I do ever figure out how the song ends,
I know it won't be with Taylor glaring at me.

"What do you want me to say?"

She groans. "Something helpful!"

I toss my journal into my backpack.
"Do you want to know what's going on in *my* life?"

She rolls her eyes. "Come on, Lily,
don't be so dramatic."

> I used to find it funny, you know.
> The way she rolls her eyes and scoffs
> at every little thing.
> But it's really not that funny.

"Can you stop calling me Lily?
        You know that's not my name, right?
You started calling me that when we were four
and now everyone just calls me that,
and I have to, what? Live with it?"

Her eyebrows shoot up. "Whoa.
What the hell is wrong with you?"

I get up to leave. "Nothing."

Nothing.   Nothing.

        Nothing.

Nothing.   Nothing.

                Nothing. Nothing.

Nothing. Nothing. Nothing.   Nothing.

I spend most of rehearsal with the stage crew kids
and Clarence, church maintenance guy
        and potentially the oldest man on Earth.

He takes us down to the basement
to pull out props and costumes from previous years
and to clear up some of the cobwebs.
                "Since we're here!"

When we finally return to the chapel,
Sister Tammy is already having the actors
run through a scene.

The Crucifixion.

Derek stands at center stage, flanked by Landon and Nalu,
as they practice holding up their arms like crosses.

Though on the actual night they'll be standing in front of
huge crucifixes with foam nails, spray-painted silver,
jutting out of their wrists.
        They'll wear swaddling clothes,
        and fake blood will drip down their skin.
Sister Tammy prides herself on accuracy
over everything.

It's always gruesome,
but the crowd can never get enough.

I watch the end of rehearsal
in the last row of pews by myself.

When Sister Tammy isn't looking,
Damien passes behind the three other boys
and jams his thumb into his brother's side, cracking up
when Derek flips him off,

and I realize that the yellow-haired boy
I thought I loved
was just a story
I made up,

and that there's another boy—
one with star eyes,
one who's real,
one who's looking right at me,
even though I'm not the girl
he's supposed to be looking at.

I'm waiting for Kāia after rehearsal
on the front steps outside church.

It's a particularly cold night, but I don't want to wait inside,
so I pull my hoodie over my head
            and try to remember what the sun feels like.

"There you are."
                                    Shit.
Nalu plops down next to me, rubbing his hands together.
"I'll never get used to this." His breath billows out
with every word.
"Waimea is cold, but this is *cold.*"

He laughs.

I nod,

unsure of what he wants me to say,
figuring it's best just to say   nothing.

"Okay." Nalu turns to face me. "What's wrong?
You've been acting weird since Sunday and dodging my texts, too."
His voice takes a sharp edge
            that I've only heard from him once.

I close my eyes,
because it's too much.

Taylor.
Tia.
Him.
Dad.
Gina Gina Gina Gina.
Derek.
It's *all* too much.

"*Hey.*" His edge softens.

I keep my eyes closed, because I know
if I look at him now—

I shake my head.
"It's nothing."

I can hear him breathing, feel him watching me when

his arm drapes over my shoulders, and the warmth
of his body radiating through the layers
between us draws from me a single tear
I don't even bother to hide,
slipping down
my
face.

"I don't know what's going on,
but I do know that the longer you hold it in
the louder it will scream
to get out."

I think
about
what
Nalu
said
for
the
rest
of
the
night.

Turning
it
over

and

examining
it
from
every
angle.

Memory

Three Months Ago

It's Christmas,
and the Greater Seattle Area is experiencing
a record-breaking snowstorm that's closed all the roads
and taken the power out for days.

Which means no three-hour-long Christmas mass.
An honest-to-goodness Christmas *miracle.*

All four of us, even Dad, decide to stay in our pajamas
to gather by the Christmas tree.

Mama lights candles, placing them all throughout the house,
and I love the way the flickering lights
make shadow shapes on our faces.

There is no body of Christ here.
No blood of him, either.

Just fistfuls of dry cereal
and a game of Yahtzee—

> I've always liked the sound the dice make
> when I seal the cup with my palm to shake.

click-de-da-clack-clack
click-de-da-clack-clack
click-de-da-clack-clack
click-de-da-clack-clack
click-de-da-clack-clack
click-de-da-clack-clack
click-de-da-clack-clack
click-de-da—

"Just throw, already!" Kāia whines,
and so

I let

the dice fly

unpredictable,

wild, and crashing,

hoping
and praying
that I land something lucky.

March 19

Solemnity of Saint Joseph, the husband of the Virgin Mary

The Perfect Husband.
Oh, Saint Joseph,
what a real
gem
you
are.
It's pretty neat
how you
didn't
ditch Mary
back there, but
what do you expect?

A cookie?
A gold star?
A parade?
For just being a decent guy?

Come *on*, dude.

When I wake up, I know it's time
to finally tell Mama
about Gina Gina Gina.
Even though she never really hears me,
I will make her listen.

Nalu is right.
The noise is
just
too
loud, and it's only getting
louder.

I try to focus on other things—
        on the carpet beneath my bare feet,
        on the *drip drip drip* of the coffee maker,
        on the whoosh of Kāia's blow-dryer,
        on the low rumble of Dad's voice on the phone
                before he leaves for work,
        on the smooth wood grain against my knuckles
        when I knock on my parents' bedroom door—
instead
of the roar erupting
through the hole in my chest.

Aren't mothers supposed to be easy to talk to?
I can't even ask mine for tampons
without flipping inside out from the embarrassment.

So how am I—

                What do I—

How do I even begin to tell her about Gina
Gina
Gina
Gina
Gina
Gina
Gina?

"You okay?" Mama asks.
I find her in her bathroom, combing coconut oil through
her hair to make her curls soft and defined
like spirals of fine silk thread. "Aouli?"

She starts to wash her hands beneath a running stream
of steaming water that beats her skin red,

and I know I need to tell her now
but the words are going

click-de-da-clack-clack around in my brain
until I
finally
let
them
fly

hoping and praying

that I land something lucky.

My mother's silence
has never been

so loud.

"I know,"
she finally says.
I know
I know
I know
I know
I know
I know
I know
I know

she can't expect me
to breathe
in this house,

that demands so much
but gives so little

its crumbling foundation
doing nothing
to keep me
from
f
a
l
l
i
n
g.

"Get off the floor, Aouli."
Mama sounds mad.
"Get up. Your father, he's going to think—"

What, Mama?

The ground has already opened up beneath me.
The earth is already trying to swallow me whole.

What could he possibly think
that could be worse than that?

"He's going to think something is wrong."

The conversation that breaks me.

Mama: Nothing is wrong.

Me: Okay.

Mama: Don't say anything.

Me: Okay.

Mama: It's complicated.

Me: Okay.

Mama: Grown-up stuff. Stuff you can't understand.

Me: Okay.

Mama: Don't tell your sister.

Me: Okay.

Mama: You cannot tell your sister.

Me: Okay.

Mama: Now get up off the floor, Aouli.

Me: Okay.

Mama: Go finish the dishes; you got to go to school soon.

Me: Okay.

Mama: You know how Dad gets when you don't do what you're supposed to.

Me: Okay, Mama.

March 21

Lenten Saturday

"Aunty 'Ehu isn't feeling well this morning," Mama says.
"So we're just going to hang out at home today."

We're in the kitchen, and Mama acts like nothing is wrong.
She sips coffee like everything is normal, like she didn't
use her own hands to rip the hole in my chest open
wide. She stands next to the window,
watching gray clouds simmer
overhead until the sky

splits open and

rains hell

down

upon

us.

Texts

2:17 p.m.

Nalu: Hey

Nalu: How are you doing today?

Me: *Typing . . .*

Me:

I pull out my song journal
and thumb through the pages
to the place I last left off.

something (still) unfinished

I ~~have~~ had this dream that I ~~can~~ could fly
that I ~~have~~ had wings to touch the sky
~~maybe someday one day~~
~~I will finally soar high~~ but before I got too high
it all came crashing down

I woke up in my bed at home
frustrated I should have known
I still have sins to atone

all that's lost resounds
all my loss resounds

March 25

The Annunciation of the Lord

A message from the angel Gabriel to Mary:
I know this must all come as a shock.
Mother of *God's* baby?
Wild. I know.

But here's the thing.
Suuuuuure, did you have big dreams?
Maybe get out of Nazareth?
Take a gap year?
Meet a cute guy? Or a few?
Joseph's great, but options are better.
Maybe you wanted to party it up in Damascus?
Or go on a beach vacay down the Red Sea coast?
I got a crazy story about that place, by the way.

Here's the thing, babe.
I know it sucks,
but you just gotta do
what you gotta do sometimes.

So be a good girl
and just do what your dad told you, okay?

Rehearsal runs long for the actors tonight,
so when I'm finished painting backdrops,
I sit in the pews and watch my sister bow at Derek's feet.

When the scene is over, he helps her up to stand
and whispers something in her ear that makes her blush.
The urge to boo and hiss at them is overwhelming.

Sister Tammy takes the microphone at the priest's podium.
"That's all for tonight, folks! See you Sunday!"

Kāia skips down from the dais to meet me.
"Ready to go?" she asks, before taking one look,
one *actual* look at me. "Are you okay?"

No, sister. I am not.

"Oh, I'm peachy."

"Hey, K!" Kāia and I turn in sync
as Derek jogs down the aisle toward us.

Tonight he's wearing a Notre Dame T-shirt that stretches
tight across his chest (tight like he-bought-a-size-too-small-
on-purpose kind of tight).

I heard he applied early action and got in—
good
fucking
riddance.

He stops a step too close to us
for comfort. "We're still on for tomorrow?"

I tense.
          Kāia melts. "Definitely."

"Great." He brushes his hand against her arm
before turning his smile on me. "Have a good night." He winks.

Then he's gone

                                        and something in me cracks.

Like I'm a little kid again
          itching for ways to annoy her,
I flick my sister on the cheek to get her attention.
"What was that? He can't even learn your name?"

Kāia crosses her arms over her chest. "It's a *nickname*."

"He's reduced you down to a single letter," I point out.
"And you're seeing him tomorrow?
Where?
Does Mama know? Does *Dad*?"

She takes a deep breath through her nose,
her eyes fluttering closed
before flicking back open. "You're being ridiculous."

"Kāia, Derek is not—"

"I know you're into him," she cuts me off. "I mean,
why wouldn't you be?"

I don't even realize who she's talking about,
not until her gaze goes all dreamy.

And that's when I start to see red.

"You think I'm into *him*?"

"I mean, you're into a lot of guys these days.
Damien. Derek. *Nalu*."
She counts them off on her fingers,
pressure building behind my eyes
with each
tick,
tick,
tick.
"Just stop letting your issues get in my way.
It's exhausting."

I reel back like she's hit me.

She might as well have.

It probably would have hurt less.

I can feel everyone's eyes on us,
see them leaning in to listen.

I don't care;

let them see

who we really are.

"What is that supposed to mean?" I ask,
shocked by how much her words hurt.

The delicate curve of her jawbone jumps,
her skin taut as a finely tuned guitar string.
"What do I mean?" A shadow falls across her face, like a cloud
passing across the sun and snuffing out all the light.
"I mean that the world doesn't revolve around *you*!
Throwing yourself at multiple guys. Fighting with Taylor.
Yelling at Dad when he and Mama are arguing
like that's ever going to solve
anything.
Jumping
out
of
a
freaking
window!

You don't get a free pass to be a bitch
just because something inside you is broken."

Those still in the nave stare at us openly.

"Is everything okay?"
Sister Tammy approaches us slowly,
like we're dangerous animals at the zoo
that have escaped from our cages.

Nalu's eyes find mine
right
as
the
first
tear
starts
to
fall—

I need to get out of here.

Now.

I pivot quickly on my heel
and walk out of the chapel.

And I don't stop,
even when my sister yells at me to come back.

I don't know

where I am going.
I'm just walking out
of the nave into the narthex
through the double doors,
down the stairs, past Saint Peter,
until I'm half way across
the parking lot and I
remember that my
jacket is still inside,
and that Kāia is
my ride, and that
my best friend isn't
my best friend
anymore and that the guy
I'm pretty sure I'm in love
with is already with
someone else, and that
Mama has no
interest in helping me mend
this jagged hole in my chest.

Kāia is right.

I

am

broken.

At the farthest edge of the parking lot,
there is nowhere left to go
but
up.

I throw my arms out wide and tilt my face toward the night sky—
        clear, vast, and starry,
        perfect for flying—

and I wait for the wind
to take me away,

but the air is   still

and I remain
unmoved.

Nalu's truck pulls up alongside me,
slowing
to a soft
brake.

My arms
sink to my sides
as the window rolls down.

"Need a ride?" Nalu hangs his arm out,
his hand dangling loose.

I can't bring myself to meet his eyes. "No."

"Jesus, Aouli," he groans. "Come on."

"No—"

"Just get in the fucking car; it's freezing out here."
His anger comes on suddenly, startling me,
but it dissipates just as quickly.
"Please. I think your sister left already."

"I said *no*." I finally turn to face him head-on.
"Don't you think you should be worrying more
about your girlfriend getting home than about me, anyway?"

And of all of the things I could have said—

this was the worst.

Nalu's mouth gapes open.
"What the hell are you talking about?"

And suddenly, I feel a lot less confident
than I did just seconds earlier.

"Well, I know you and Tia are . . ." I shift uneasily
from foot to foot. "I know you two are together—"

Nalu silences me with a frustrated sound.
"Well, that makes one of us, Aouli."

"Taylor said—"

"Yeah, it sounds like Taylor says a lot of shit."
He pinches the bridge of his nose, his eyes shuttering closed.

"What are you saying?" I take one step toward the truck
with something like hope stirring in my chest.

He speaks so quietly, barely loud enough for me to hear
him over the hum of the engine.

"What I'm saying is that I like *you,* Aouli.

A lot."

I open my mouth, eager
to tell him

I'm sorry.
I messed up.
Let me make this better.
I like you, too. So. Much.
I'm falling for you.
I know we've only known each other for a little while,
but it's true.

But I don't get to say any of that.

"Ignoring me and giving me the cold shoulder, though?"
Nalu scratches the back of his head. "It's gotten old, really fast."

I take a step toward him, fingers twitching at my sides. "Nalu—"

"I just wish you could get out of your own way; maybe then
you would understand."

He gazes out his window, up at the sky.

"Everything was so dark after Mom died,
but then I met you
and I could finally see the stars again."

"Go back inside, Aouli."
Nalu jerks
his chin
toward
the church,
and without
another word,

he's gone.

Dad has to pick me up
because Nalu was right
and my sister did leave without me,

because I don't have wings
and the wind never came to carry me away.

Dad is already grumbling
before I even get my seat belt on.

"You need to be nicer to your sister."

Of course he assumes what happened
between us was all my fault—

maybe it was a little.

Whatever.
Let him grumble.

I have
no more
fight left
in me tonight.

Dad is quiet for the entirety of the ride
through Hawk Valley,
past the grocery store,
past the fire station,
past the hair salon Mama's gone to for years,
past the winding road to Taylor's house,
past the park where Dad taught me to ride a bike,
down the cut through the forest—
the one that feels like flying—
past my elementary school and the sidewalk
that leads straight home,
and into our little neighborhood,
where the houses all look the same,

he is quiet
all
the
way,

until—

"You need to make sure you look out
for your sister, too," he says suddenly,

as if we had been talking this entire time.

"She's fine, Dad."

She's not broken

like me.

"Just promise me, Aouli."
"Why?"

"Just—"

"Fine. I promise."

"Kāia's not as tough as you."
I blink slowly, trying to make sense
of what he's telling me.

He turns into the driveway,
and we sit in silence together, watching
the garage door roll up slowly.

"How do you know?" I look at him,

but his eyes refuse to meet mine.
"Because I made you tough. Tough like me."

March 28

Lenten Saturday

Dream

Aunty ʻEhu waits for me.
Rocking back
                                        and forth
in a wicker chair.

"Aouli." She smiles. "I hoped you would be here."

Swirling fog embraces us
from all sides, obscuring the view,
but I know where we are.

I can smell the sharp, upturned earth,
the after-rain, dew-tipped grass,
the sweet pungency of pīkake.

I'm in Waimea.
At my tūtū and papa's house.

        The house below the mountain
        and above the sea.

        The house my father was raised in.

I'm home.

Dream

"What's going on, Aunty?"
I take a seat at her feet like we used to as kids
when she would tell us old stories,
like the one about the boy who turned to stone,
or the cautionary tale of the sneaky mo'o who lives on a river,
or my favorite, about Hi'iaka and Lohi'au,
and how they fell in love despite Pele's jealousy.

"I'm waiting." Aunty 'Ehu rocks back and forth,
back and forth, back and forth. "For my brother.
He should be here soon." She looks off
at something in the distance
through the fog
to a place
I cannot
see. "Very soon."

A flock of crows shoot out of the clouds
and their cries sound like

"Soon."
"Soon."
"Soon." "Soon."
"Soon."
"Soon."

Memory

One Year Ago

Papa—my grandfather—taught me how to fly.
He would pick me up and throw me in the air
            with his strong brown arms
            that were good for flinging and made for catching.

He showed me
how to reach my hands up,
how to touch the sky,
how to brush the clouds with my nose,
how to beckon the sun,
how to take my place among the stars—

but Papa is gone, I have to remind myself,

as Dad and I stand in front of a casket
adorned with ropes of twisting ti leaf leis.

Dad holds my hand
tightly in his,
as we send Papa off with a pule,
to   wherever it is   souls go
when their time on Earth is through.

Dream

I think Papa will be here soon.

Honk! Honk!

I know that sound. That's his truck,
but I can't see through the fog
boiling over
every
edge,
seeping through
every crack.

Aunty 'Ehu stands with ease,
no sigh, no groan of frustration, but quick
like she is young again. "Time to go."

I hurry onto my feet, ready to go with her,
but she stops me.

"Eh, eh, eh. Not you, honey girl."

Dream

Headlights

break through

the fog

searching searching searching.

Papa came back
for us,
for me.

Papa wouldn't leave me

here,

not without

my wings.

Dream

A crow dives from the flock,
and I realize

I

know

her.

'Alalā, my 'aumakua, my protector, the one
from Aunty 'Ehu's prayers, the one
from Dad's bedtime story, the one
from my dreams.

With her black wings thrown wide,
she dips and flips and spins,
landing with a *whoosh* of her feathers onto Aunty ʻEhu's shoulder.

"Soon!" "Soon!" "Soon!"

Dream

Aunty ʻEhu starts to leave.

"Goodbye, Aouli," and now,
she is the fog.

"I love you, Aouli," and now,
she is the sea.

"Be brave, Aouli," and now,
she is the mountain.

"Don't forget, Aouli," and now,
she is ʻAlalā.

"Look to our ancestors.
They guide the way," and now,
she soars
higher and higher and higher until I can't see her anymore—

"But what about me?" I ask the fog.

"Don't forget about me!" I scream to the sea.

"Aunty, please!" I beg the mountain.

"Don't leave me," I whisper to 'Alalā. "Don't leave."

Dream

Papa's headlights grow

brighter and

brighter and

brighter

until everything is unflinching light
and 'Alalā circling—

and just as his truck

b r e a k s

through the fog

I

wake

up.

Part Three

I am the resurrection and the life.

John 11:25

March 29

Palm Sunday of the Passion of the Lord

The entire house smells
like sugar pushed too far to the edge,
          like something is burning.

"Dad?"

He's alone in the kitchen, standing at the stove,
staring at three pancakes burning black in the griddle.

"Dad?" Panic rises in my voice. "What's wrong?"

"Aunty 'Ehu—" he starts, only to cut off abruptly,
struggling to tell me what Aunty 'Ehu
already told me herself last night.

She's gone she's gone she's gone she's gone.

"Dad, let me." He jumps at my touch,
when I put my hand on his back to turn off the stove
and lift the griddle off the burner.

I let the weight of it in my hands pin me to this moment
before dumping the pancakes in the trash and shutting the lid,

even though I know
          the smell of burned sugar
                    always   lingers.

slender
rough palm
in my palm
raised to the ceiling

four mourning souls
in the back row
palms stuck up

pleading
praying
begging

for resurrection

Dad still makes us
go to Stations of the Cross rehearsal,

and no one notices the hole in my chest.
    That it keeps getting bigger, that soon
    there won't be enough of me left
    to patch back together.

I think Nalu tries to talk to me, but I'm not really here.
I think he tries.
I think I push him   away.

Taylor doesn't even try, but it is for the best.

If she asked
if I was okay,
and if I had to open my mouth, I have no idea

what

would

spill

out.

In
between
Stations,
Kāia
rests
her
shoulder
against
mine,
and
I
let
her

use
me
to
prop
herself
up.
I
hold
all
of
her
weight,
and
the
grief
that's
made
her
heavy,
because
I
don't
think
I
could
stay
upright
on
my

own
anyway,
if
she
decided
to
pull
away.

When Kāia and I get home after rehearsal,
the house is silent as death.

Dad is holed up in his office.

Mama has locked herself away in her bathroom.

Kāia withdraws to her bedroom, mumbling something
about a test she has to study for.

I retreat to my own bedroom alone
and wind up in bed with the covers pulled up to my chin,
wishing more than anything that I could talk to Nalu—

not that I have any idea what I would even say.

I feel heavy,
like my bones have turned to stone.
That if I lie here long enough
maybe they will drag me
down
down
down
down
through the mattress
through the box spring
through the spot in the carpet never reached by a vacuum
through the foundation of the house
and straight
into
the
earth.

I burrow deeper into my quilt
and roll over onto my side,
            coming nose to leather
with the soft corner of my song journal
sitting on my nightstand.

I haven't touched it since last week
after finding myself stuck on what came next.

I open up to my unfinished song
and read what I wrote,

feel the pain I inked into the page with each line,
squeeze my eyes shut when I'm reminded

of how much worse
everything is now—

and then I realize

I know what to say.

I never had much interest
in learning how to play an instrument,
despite Dad's prodding to get me
to pick up the piano or the violin because
"it looks good on college applications;
nobody's going to care if you can sing,
especially not our kine music,
trust me."
But I didn't listen, of course.
I always thought my voice was enough on its own.

With my finger hovering over the record button,
I can only pray that it is.

Texts

6:00 p.m.

Me: I know you wanted to hear what I had so far so

I don't let myself think about it.
I just hit send.

Me: unfinished.mp3

I stay up all night,

but his response

never

comes.

March 30

Monday of Holy Week

I'm miserable at school
all day, agonizing over my mistake,
imagining Nalu playing my stupid, *stupid* recording
for his friends and all of them
laughing
at my pathetic
attempt
to show him
the hole in my chest.

Students, high on the *riiing riiing riiing* of the final bell,
buzz all around me, their chatter like static in my ear.

The parking lot after school is always a mess,
but today it feels especially difficult to navigate,
    as I try to remember where Kāia parked
    this morning, scanning for her used sedan
    in a sea of used sedans,   when—
the sound of my name,
complete, full, and perfect all on its own,
stops me
in my
tracks.

"Aouli!"

Nalu stands in front of his truck,
waiting
for
me
in his white-and-navy St. Joseph's uniform
with the tie tugged loose
and the top three buttons of his shirt undone.
He offers me a small wave, but I'm stuck
where I stand, convinced that my mind is playing tricks on me.

Even when I'm standing in front of him,
I can't believe it.

"What are you doing here?"

He doesn't answer right away. He seems nervous,
fussing with his hair, raking his hand back so it all sticks up
in different directions.

"I listened to your song."

My stomach drops, and I brace
myself for whatever he's going to say next.

"I loved it, and I know it's not finished yet,
but I really hope you finish it,
I mean, you should definitely finish it,
and I'm sorry I didn't respond, but I didn't know what to say,
so I came here and now that I'm here I realize
I should have texted first, so I'm sorry if this feels weird

and I can go if you want me to go,
I just thought—"

I don't let him finish.
I throw my arms around him, cutting
him off. "No, don't go."

And when he hugs me back
that's when I come
undone.

I force myself to pull away
when I notice all the people staring
at us laced together in the middle of the parking lot.

I sniff and wipe my nose with the back of my hand.
Gross. But who the hell cares?
Nalu is *here*.

"Could we, uh, go somewhere else?"

Nalu nods. "Sure, of course. Where?"

I shrug. "Anywhere but here?"

He smiles. "Yeah, I've got the perfect place,
actually."

A conversation on the road out of Hawk Valley.

Me: So where are you taking me?

Nalu: Well, whenever I feel down, I always end up in the same place.

Me: And where's that?

Nalu: Church.

Me: Okay, I know you're new here, but St. Peter's is in the opposite direction.

Me: And no offense, but that's kind of the last place I want to be right now.

Nalu: We're not going to St. Peter's.

Me: But you just said—

Nalu: You'll see. Just hold tight; it's a bit of a drive.

Nalu: But it's worth it.

When Nalu pulls into the parking lot,
I know where we are immediately,
even though I haven't been here in years. "*This* is church for you?"

"Just trust me," he says, putting his truck in park.

And I do, I really do.

Memory

Thirteen Years Ago

Kāia and I aren't old enough
to go to school yet, so we spend our days
with Mama.

She takes us all the way up to Gene Coulon Park
on the south shore of Lake Washington
to dip our toes in the freezing water,
to play chase around the playground,
to watch the geese make arrows in the sky.

All three of us end up squished together side by side
like sardines, trying to fit on the small quilt
Mama brought from home.

"It's not Hawai'i," Mama says. "But let's close our eyes
and listen to the water and pretend it is,
just for a little bit."

The entrance to the park still boasts
the same blue-and-yellow sign I remember
from my time spent here as a kid.

COULON BEACH PARK
This Park Provided by the
Citizens of Renton

We walk along the paved path to the beach
and the park is humming with life, a sign that spring
might finally be on its way.

An elderly man throws breadcrumbs at the seagulls,
despite all the signs begging parkgoers:
PLEASE DO NOT FEED THE BIRDS.

A woman runs past with her dog leashed
to her hip, the sound of her calculated breathing
muddling with the sound of her dog's loud panting.

A group of kids, younger than us but old enough
to be without their parents, sit together in the grass,
laughing with their heads thrown back.

"So what god do you worship here?" I ask Nalu,
as we arrive at the edge of the beach.

He swings his arm across my shoulders,
like it's the most natural thing in the world.
Grinning wide, he tugs me closer.
"The sky."

Nalu lets me
tell him every story
I have about Aunty 'Ehu

until I've laughed a little
        and cried a lot,

until the sun starts to dip
        and the sky is orange and pink,

but I don't tell him
about Dad, about Gina, about Mama, about Kāia
                because
                it's
                still
                too
                much.

"Everything just feels really bad right now," I say instead,
into my open palms lying limply in my lap.
"And it feels like it's all my fault."

Nalu waits a beat before asking me,
"Do you want to know why I call this church?"

"Why?"

"I've gone to church my whole life.
My parents, too.
My grandparents.
Their grandparents.
But before that, things were different for us."

And I know by *us*, he means Hawaiians.
And it feels so good to be the same as him.

Then I think of what Aunty 'Ehu told me.
About the gods that live all around us.
About our ancestors.
About 'Alalā.

"I always struggled to buy into church,
and then my mom died—"
He pauses for a split second,
clearing his throat before continuing.
"And then I *really* didn't buy into it anymore.
It just doesn't make sense to me,
the idea that there is only good or evil
or that bad things only happen because you deserve them."
He leans into me, and his shoulder against mine
feels like growing roots deep into the earth,
right here beside the water.
"Or that when someone dies
they leave for good to some faraway paradise,
when I swear there isn't a day that's gone by since her death
that I haven't felt my mom like she's standing right next to me.

I feel nothing when I'm at church," he says softly,
the slightest edge of guilt in his voice.
"But when I'm outside, looking at the sky over the water,
I feel *everything*."

The sky is awash with color
as the sun sets in a bright blaze
over the mountains.
The last of daylight beckons in the night,
the beauty in both joining together
for one spectacular show.

I set my hands down in the cool sand
that is rough and coarse, unlike the fine golden grains
along the Kona coast.

"You know Aunty 'Ehu never went to church?
My dad tried to get her to go with us so many times,
but she always said no."

"Really?" Nalu chuckles, looking out
across the smooth surface of the water.

"I used to think it was because she didn't like to be told
what to do, but now I wonder
if it was because she already believed
in something bigger?"

My phone keeps buzzing in my pocket,
and I know I can't afford to ignore my family
any longer.

I sigh, dusting off the back of my jeans as I stand.
"I should probably go. My dad's head might actually
be exploding right now."

"Let's go, then." Nalu reaches up to me.
"Help me up first?"

I grip his hand in mine
and pull hard until we're standing

chest to chest—

how can I bring myself to worry anymore
about what is waiting for me at home

when Nalu won't stop looking at me like *that,*
like I am art and worthy of marveling over?

On the walk back to the car,
we take our time,
neither of us rushing
the other.

Dusk has settled over the park,
painting everything blue.

Nighttime critters awaken,
their chitters and chirps rising out of the brush,
        comforting as a lullaby.

Music is everywhere,
if you know how to listen for it.

As we approach his truck, I slow to a halt.
        "I want to apologize."
I stare down at the tops of my sneakers,
unable to bring myself to look him in the eye.
"For everything I said the other night after rehearsal.
It was messed up of me to be mad at you
for something you didn't even do."

Nalu nods in agreement. "It was messed up."

Then,

with the gentlest touch,

he cups my cheek,

encouraging me to meet his gaze.

"But I forgive you."

Nalu parks three houses down from mine
at my request.

I know I need to get out, but I'm not ready
to face Dad just yet.

As if he can read my mind,
Nalu kills the engine and weaves his fingers
through mine.

"I'm sorry for keeping you so long," he murmurs,
but I can't concentrate on what he's saying

because the way his thumb brushes
across the back of my hand
feels like flying,
and I'm going
up
up
up
like a rocket, blasting through
the stratosphere.
"I hope I didn't get you in trouble."

Oh, but I already am
in so so *so* much
trouble.

Yep. I got in trouble.
For running off.
For not telling Kāia.
For not answering my phone.
For being in a boy's car without permission.
For not being a good daughter.
For not being a good sister.
For not being good enough.
But *ohmygod* it was so worth it.

Dear ʻAlalā,
If I am your descendant,
and you have wings,
does that mean
that I might have
wings,
too?

ʻĀmene.

April 1

Wednesday of Holy Week

Tonight is the last rehearsal
for Stations of the Cross
before the performance on Saturday night.

Which means costumes, music, and lighting
to make sure everything is in order.
So while the actors practice their parts,
I practice mine.

I work with the other stage crew members in the dark
between each station to change the sets and switch out props
and to *most importantly*
make sure the crucifixes are secure when the time comes.

A criminal's cross fell a few years ago
because someone didn't double-check it was locked
into the base.

It was hilarious.

Don't worry, he was *fine*.

As we near the end of the final run-through,
Sister Tammy makes me switch crucifix-securing duties
with another member of the stage crew.

"Brady will be in charge of Landon's cross
since he's already on the left side of the stage.
So *you* will be in charge of Nalu's now."

Nalu snags my attention from where he
waits beside the dais
and winks at me—
I'm dying.
I'm dead.
I'm *done*.

It's time to rehearse the main event,
when Jesus and the criminals are nailed to their crosses.
    Which *means*
    it's time for Sister Tammy's Big Lecture,
    the same lecture she has to give every year.

"Now, I expect you will all be mature
and show respect to your classmates.
Remember,
this
is
a
holy
show!"
She waits for everyone to nod before
signaling to the guys. "Okay, boys."

Derek, then Landon, and finally Nalu
all take off their long tunics so they're standing
in nothing but short white wraps.

And there is only a split second of silence
before someone
lets out a long whistle—

"What. Did. I. Say!"

Sister Tammy's knuckles turn white,
gripping the sides of her clipboard.

Landon flexes,
earning a few stray hoots from his friends.

Derek just looks smug,
like he knows everyone is looking at him.

And Nalu,
he's all dark and lean lines,
strong legs,
steady shoulders,
humble tilt to his chin—

he's beautiful
he's beautiful
he's beautiful
he's beautiful.

I think I've forgotten how to breathe
        when someone clicks their tongue,
        startling me back to reality.

Between the tunics coming off
and Nalu quite literally taking my breath away,
August appeared with an armful of cords—
        was he asking me for my help?

        I think he might have been,

but honestly,

who can hear anything in here

with Nalu standing there
looking like *that*.

I cross my arms. "What?"

August rolls his eyes. "You're drooling."

"I am not." I yank the cords out of his grasp.
"And give me those."

"Lily?"
Everyone turns their head to
look
at
me.

August chuckles under his breath.
I panic as a few snickers float out of the group.
"What? I mean—"

Sister Tammy waves her arms at me.
"Lily, are you paying attention?"

I squeeze my eyes closed
for a nanosecond. "Yeah?"

"We're switching stations, so let's go."
She twirls her fingers, one around the other.

"Right! *Right.*" I pass the cords back to August,
forgetting why I even took them in the first place,
then hurry to the base of Nalu's cross as the rest of the transition
between stations continues.

I don't look at him.
I refuse to look at him.
I can't look at him because surely
if I do,
if I dare,
my skin will turn to flame.

"You forgot about me?" Nalu teases,
and I can practically hear the smile in his voice.

"Shut *up.*"

April 3

Good Friday

Texts

8:31 p.m.

Me: My dad just told us Aunty ʻEhu's funeral isn't going to happen until spring break, so Kāia and I can actually go

Me: Can you believe he wasn't going to let us if we were going to miss school????

Nalu: That would have sucked

Me: Seriously.

Me: Are you going to Kona for the funeral too?

Nalu: Yep. I'll be close to you too, my tūtū lives down the street from yours apparently.

Me: Really??? I wonder if we ever met as kids?

Nalu: I was just wondering the same thing.

Nalu: Pretty sure I would remember you though.

12:00 a.m.

Me: I'm glad you're going to be there.

Me: In Kona.

Nalu: Go to sleep, Aouli.

12:33 a.m.

Nalu: I'm glad you're going to be there too

April 4

Holy Saturday

Tonight is the big night,
but we are running late
because of me.

What can I say?

At least I'm consistent.

As soon as Kāia and I get to the church,
I try to find Nalu to wish him good luck,
but Sister Tammy shoos me out of the actors' area
in the basement before I can see him.

"You should be upstairs already!
Go go, go!"

Texts

6:35 p.m.

Me: Tried to say hi to you but Sister Tammy freaked

Nalu: She takes this really seriously yeah?

Me: Lol what gave it away

Me: Was it her color-coded minute by minute schedule?

Me: Or maybe it was the 2am emails in all caps that she sent this morning?

Nalu: Hahahaha

Nalu: It's the makeup actually

Nalu: I knew about the fake blood, but I didn't realize she would make me wear foundation and eyeliner

Me: Hot

Nalu: I do look pretty good

Nalu: When I asked her why I needed it she accused me of not wanting to be a real actor.

Me: That's show biz baby

It feels like the entire parish is here tonight
when I peek out from backstage—
which isn't so much a backstage
as it is a wide hallway hidden behind the dais—
to get a good look at the audience
chattering quietly with those around them.

The nave is dark, except for the spotlight shining on the dais,
which has been cleared of the altar, the podium,
and the priest's and deacon's chairs to act as our stage.

I spot Mama and Dad sitting in the front row
with the Tuigamalas and Nalu's dad and sister.

When Keala catches me peeking,
she gives me a thumbs-up, and I offer a wave in return.

From far away,
my parents look normal.
Happy, even.
And I mourn what we could have been.
What I could have been.
Something soft, gentle, quiet.

But what if?

A small voice in my head urges me to reconsider
that maybe I was never meant to be something expected.

Maybe I was meant to be something more.

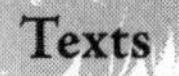

Texts

6:55 p.m.

Nalu: Are you and Kāia coming to Katie's party tonight?

Me: I doubt she was really inviting us. Her parents probably made her

Me: You St. Joe's kids are very exclusive you know

Nalu: -_-

Nalu: Well I heard her parents won't even be there, just her older sister so

Nalu: Pleaseeeeeee come

Me: Ugh

Me: Our dad won't let us go

Nalu: Tell him I'm going!

Me: I don't think that would work out the way you think

Nalu: :(

Me: I will ask but no promises!

Nalu: :)

Sister Tammy is sweating
from running back and forth backstage.
"Lily, put your phone away!" she snaps.
"The show is about to start!"

The spotlight shining on the stage dims
as Sister Tammy's voice—which is suddenly calm and pleasant—
erupts out of the speakers.

"Welcome, family and friends, to the St. Peter's Youth Group presentation

of the Stations of the Cross."

Station | Jesus Is Condemned to Death

"Hey." Nalu appears behind me,
and the heat of his body so close to mine
sends me into a tailspin.

I am condemned
to suffer
beneath
the weight of every
indecent thought that rushes into my brain
as I hand Nalu the nails for his wrists and he whispers low,
"Don't forget about me out there."

As if I could ever forget him?

A bird without its wings
still dreams of flying,
doesn't it?

"Death!"
Damien, as Pontius Pilate,
yells onstage.

"Death to the impostor messiah!"

Station | Jesus Must Bear the Cross

Gina

Gina

Gina

Gina

Gina

Dad Mama Kāia Dad Mama Kāia Dad Mama Kāia Dad Mama

Dad Mama Kāia Dad Mama Kāia Dad Mama Kāia Dad Mama

Dad Mama Kāia Dad Mama Kāia Dad Mama Kāia Dad Mama

Gina

Gina

Gina

Gina

Gina

Gina

Gina

Gina

Gina

Gina

Gina

Gina

Gina

Gina

Gina

Gina

Gina

Derek Taylor Derek Taylor Derek Taylor Derek Taylor

Derek Taylor Derek Taylor Derek Taylor Derek Taylor

I have never been strong enough
for the cross
I must bear
on
my
back.

Onstage, Derek rises with the cross.

It is weightless, made of foam,
but he still makes a good show
of straining his muscles.

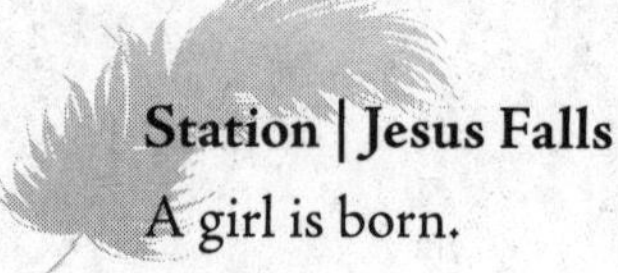

Station | Jesus Falls

A girl is born.

Not promised.
Not destined.
Not a savior.

But with holes
in her back
where wings
should have
sprouted.

A girl is born.

Her only promise,
her only destiny is to

fall
fall
fall

with nothing
there to save
her.

Derek hits the floor,
and gasps erupt out of the audience,
like they don't already know
how this story ends.

Station | Jesus Meets His Mother

Hail Mary,
mother of God,
I know your secret.
You know mine, too.
That we are not just
our story—
            the one He made up.
We
are
so
much
more.
Pray for me, Mary, now
and at the hour
of my death.

Amen.

Kāia runs onstage, dressed
in virginal white, to kneel
beside Derek.

She is a good actress.
She's been practicing for this role
her whole life.

Station | Simon Helps Jesus

"Zip me up?" Taylor talks to me
 with her back turned to my face.

I wish her luck.
I tell her to break a leg.

She spins around. "Thanks."

Then I ask her to help me make sure the other girls
are ready to go.

"Ugh. Can't you just do it?" She looks at me like I am the Romans,
and she is Simon of Cyrene,
 but she has it twisted because I've been carrying her
 cross for years, and she can't even see
 that mine is killing me.

Garrett, as Simon, takes
the cross off Derek's back.

Garrett stumbles.

Station | The Women Weep

But who will cry

for us?

Taylor, Tia, Julie, Abby, and Katie
rush onto the stage and pretend to sob
at Derek's feet while he looks onto them,

pleased.

Station | Jesus Is Stripped

I am
stripped
bare

as Nalu squeezes my hand
before taking the stage,

and I swear he can see
all of me.

Wide sky.
Promised body.
Sharp heart.

Gaping holes in my back.

All of it.

Derek's tunic is removed onstage,
while Landon and Nalu emerge
bare-chested.

Station | Death

A girl is born
to pay
for the sins
of her father,

to endure
a slow tumble
toward death.

My father!
My father!

Why have you
forsaken me?

Derek's voice
fills the chapel.

"Eli! Eli!
Lema sabachthani!"

My God!
My God!

Why have you forsaken me?

The lights dim.

I dart
into the dark
to disassemble the cross,
help switch the background,
remove the crown of thorns
atop Derek's head.
I find Nalu, my feet
having memorized
the way, to take the nails
back. But when I turn
to leave—

I'm stopped
by Nalu's arm
around my waist.

Chest to chest.

Heart to heart.

Lips to lips.

And from my back,
my wings unfurl.

The lights come on.

Thump, thump.
Thump, thump.
Thump, thump.
Thump, thump.
Thump, thump.
Thump, thump.
Thump, thump.
Thump, thump.
Thump, thump.
Thump, thump.
Thump, thump.
Thump, thump.
Thump, thump.
Thump, thump.
Thump, thump.
Thump, thump.
Thump, thump.
Thump, thump.
Thump, thump.
Thump, thump.
Thump, thump.
Thump, thump.
Thump, thump.

My heart!
My heart!

I can feel my heart
again.

Station | Jesus Is Reborn

A girl is not born
to die but to
resurrect
anew.

Not a girl.
But a fearsome thing
with wings.

Derek bursts out of the tomb
that is actually just a tent,

and

the

crowd

goes

wild.

All of us file out onto the stage
to hold hands, to bow,
to accept a standing ovation from the audience.

"Juice and cookies in the narthex!" Sister Tammy announces,
as everyone disperses throughout the nave
to find their family and friends.

I hang back, watching Kāia join Mama and Dad
and wrap them both up in hugs.

I should join them.

But I know I can't. Not yet. They would know.
They would figure it out.

They would read the truth like scripture on my face.
The Devil hath taken her and kissed her mighty good.

And I can't, I can't go on pretending
that I can't fly,
now that I have my wings.

I sneak out
the back door,
tumbling into the cool night
that smells like spring,
like something new
is right on the verge
of blossoming.

I press my hand into my chest
            and try to calm my heart
as I lean back against the building,
smiling up at the sky
when
the door
opens
again—

Nalu.

Half Roman criminal.
Half star-eyed boy.

The conversation that changes everything.
Me: Hi.
Nalu: Hey.
Me: Nice job tonight—
Nalu: I'm sorry for kissing you.

Me: You are?

Nalu: Yes—

Nalu: I mean, *no*. I mean—

Nalu: I am sorry I didn't ask first.

Nalu: I am sorry if I made you uncomfortable.

Me: You didn't.

Nalu: Really?

Me: Really.

Nalu: Still. I'll ask next time.

Me: Next time?

Nalu: I'm hopeful.

Me: For?

Nalu: A next time.

Turns out
that next time
can't come
soon enough.

Wings wide.
Heart pumping.

I finally get
the kiss
I always
dreamed of.

Only

this

was

so

much

better.

"Please, Dad, *please?*"
Dad's nostrils flare. "What has gotten into you?"

My wings, Dad.

I have wings now.

We're standing outside the church—
unmoving like rocks while people flow around us
like a fast-moving river to their cars—
        and I'm begging him to let me go to Katie's party,
        while Mama and Kāia watch from the sidelines.

Dad speaks low, so no one around us hears.
"I don't know Katie,
I don't know her parents,
I don't know where she lives.
No, you are not going to this party."

Mama and I lock eyes, but she is quick
to shift her gaze away.

She hasn't really looked at me since we talked
about Gina Gina Gina Gina.

I attempt to bargain. "Two hours? Just two hours?
One hour,
what
about
one
hour?"

Dad's lips curl inward, and I brace for what I know will be a nasty scolding, when—

"What if *I* go with her?"

Kāia focuses on the rounded toes of her shiny ballet flats,
her favorite shoes.

The same ones she wears for every quiz, test,
class speech, and science project,

anytime she's hoping
for a little extra luck.

All three of our heads turn slowly to look at my sister,
and I think Dad is so shocked that he can't even muster the rage
to scold her for interrupting.

"You want to go to this party?" he asks.

Kāia sighs,
then meets his gaze.
"It's more of a casual hangout, I think."

Oh my God. I think this is the first time my sister
has ever lied to our father.

Miracles do happen.

Dad pinches the bridge of his nose, and I'm sure
he's about to say no,

but this is turning out to be an evening full of surprises.

"Fine," he agrees, shocking us all.
"One hour. That's it."

I'm *vibrating* from the
excitement,
confusion,
disbelief
all coursing through me.

Dad's eyes narrow at me,
and I worry that he might see
what's changed.

I have my wings now,
and they're beating against the bars
of my cage.

"Thanks, Dad. Just one hour."
Kāia gives him a hug,
and I swear he's gripping on to her
like if he lets go, she will sprout wings, too.

We say goodbye,
we love you,
we promise to stay together,
we promise to be safe,
we promise.

It turns out Katie lives in a mansion.

Kāia cranes her neck as she looks up
at the tall columns that frame the double-door entrance,
her eyes getting wider the higher they go.

"Oh boy."

I laugh.

Her eyebrows furrow. "What?"

"You're just the only eighteen-year-old I know
who says old-timey shit like *oh boy.*"

She clicks her tongue. "It's not old-timey."

Smiling big, I ring the doorbell. "Here we go."

Ring ding ding dinggggg ring da-ding ding ding!

Kāia sighs. "I wonder if I'll ever know what it's like
to have fancy doorbell money?"

The door swings open—

"Kylie! Laia! You made it!"

Kāia side-eyes me
as I bite back a smile.

Katie stands in the doorway and ushers us in,
spilling a little of whatever is in her cup.
"Come in, come in;
everyone is out back on the veranda."

The veranda, I mouth at my sister,
holding up my pinky when Katie's back turns.

Kāia shoves my hand down
just as Katie whips back around
to tell us,

"Oh, don't do that."

We freeze
right as we were both leaning down
to take off our shoes.

"Oh." Kāia nods quickly. "Sure."

So we keep our shoes on and follow
Katie through her house while I try
to keep my jaw from
hitting
the
floor.

Everything in here is so
white

white couches white carpet
perfect white walls— white white white.
Even Katie's wearing
all white tonight:
a velvet white miniskirt and a white crop top
that looks perfect against her perfect white skin.

And now I feel like too much in my favorite dress.
A long floral maxi that Mama bought me
for my birthday last year,

now a mistaken splatter of paint
on a canvas better left
blank.

bodiespackedtightintoanyavailablespace
musicthumpingsoloudIcanfeelitinmychest
sowekeeptotheedgeswatchingoutforspilled
drinksandboyswhotrytograbatourbacksides
anditfeelslikebeingsmushedinsideatinybox
Itellmyselfthisishowpeoplehaveagoodtime
thisisnotacagethisisnotacagethisisnotacage
eventhoughitfeelsalotlikeonethisisnotacage

Katie doesn't stick around for long
and leaves us to fend for ourselves.

"The floor is sticky!" Kāia cries in my ear.

I grab her hand, so I don't lose her to the crowd.
"Don't think about it too hard!"

I tow her through the undulating mass of bodies
as we exit the house and enter out onto the veranda,
shoving my way through
until
I finally
feel
the cool touch
of a railing
and the kiss
of fresh air
on my face
again.

Kāia sighs. "This is definitely *not*
just a youth group party."

No, it is not.

It seems that Katie has invited every upperclassman
from St. Joseph's to what was *supposedly*
a youth-group-only gathering—

but there's something about the bewildered look
on my sister's face that's so funny,
I have to laugh.

"This isn't funny, Aouli!
Dad is going to kill me,
kill *us*,
if he finds out!"

"Then don't tell him, Kylie!" I flick her nose.
"Or do you think I'm Kylie and you're Laia?"

Kāia's anxiety sharpens to frustration.

"Don't start."

"Make way! Make way!"
A tall guy with long, lanky limbs
bobs through the crowd toward us, towering over
most of the people here.

He passes out cups and pours drinks
from a big plastic jug situated atop his shoulder.
When he reaches us, he offers me a red plastic cup.

"Drink?"

"Sure!"

I go to take it,
but Kāia slaps my hand away.

"She's okay. You can move on."

I flush. "*Kāia.*"

"Chill out, damn." The guy backs away slowly.

Kāia's eyes narrow.
That gets him moving quicker.

I cross my arms. "Why did you want to come
if you don't even want to let loose a little?"

But my sister isn't listening to me.
She's busy searching,
eyes roving across all the unfamiliar faces.

Then I see
exactly why
my sister wanted
to come tonight.
I watch him

part the
crowd like
Moses did the
Red Sea.
Derek Miller
looks at my sister
like a mountain lion
looks at a deer
just
before
it
strikes.
"There you are," he says
to Kāia. "I've been looking for you."

Kāia's fantasy of Derek
plays like a free show
for anyone who
can catch a glimpse
of her hazel eyes
welling over
with awe.

"Really?" she asks, so clearly shocked,
which seems to please him immensely.

Which makes *me* want to throttle him.

"Come on, it's crazy out here."

Then he takes her hand,
leads her away,
parts   the sea
of sweaty   bodies
once   more,

and I let him.

I let him take her.
I leave her to this churning sea. I let it drown her.
And it feels like breaking a promise
I made not too long ago.

It doesn't feel right, letting her go.
But this is my one night to be free,
to let my wings spread wide.

No one is going to take this
new freedom from me.

Not Dad.
Not Mama.
Not Gina.
Not Taylor.
Not Derek.
Not Kāia.

Tonight, I'm going to soar.
Tonight, I'm going to reach the stars.

I get the attention of the guy handing out drinks,
waving him over. "Hey!"

His eyes shift back and forth, and I wonder
if he's checking to make sure Kāia is really gone.

And just the thought of that
makes me smile.

"What's up?" he asks, when he is sure
that the coast is clear.

I hold out my hand. "I'll have a drink now."

Texts
9:22 p.m.

Me: There are sooooo many people here

Me: Are you here yet?

Nalu: Walking in now!

Me: Yay!

Nalu: Where you at?

Me: Outside on the *snooty voice* veranda

Nalu: What the hell is a veranda?

Gentle fingers tangle with mine,
surprising me but not startling me,
because I know right away
who it is.

"You found me."

Nalu grins. "It took way too long
to scrub all that makeup and fake blood off."
The ends of his hair are wet,
curling as they dry.

I let go of his hand and comb my fingers
through his waves, causing his eyes to shutter briefly
and my heart to beat so loud
I'm sure he can hear it.

"I'm disappointed," I murmur.

His eyes fly back open. "Why?"

"I was kind of hoping you'd keep the eyeliner.
You should wear it more often."

He laughs, circling his arm around my waist
and tugging me closer.
"I'll wear whatever you want me to wear."

Holy moly mother of *God*.

Then Nalu kisses me
for the third time,
then the fourth time,
the fifth, and the sixth.

He kisses me outside,
surrounded by all these people.

He kisses me on the dance floor,
which is actually just the living room
with the couches pushed against the walls.

He kisses me before he leaves me
and again when he comes back with more drinks.

He kisses me until I can't decipher if it's the alcohol
or him that's making me dizzy.

He kisses me down a long hallway,
where we're finally alone.

He kisses me until I've forgotten all about my sister
and the promise I made to Dad in the car,
until all of the noise—
Dad
    Gina
        Derek
            Taylor
        Mama
Kāia—   is finally   quiet.

Eventually, Nalu and I wander up to the second floor
to escape the party racket
and talk and kiss
and explore the rest of Katie's massive house.

We wind up at the end of a hallway,
at an open window facing the forest,

because in this neighborhood the houses are not
packedtightlytogether
but separated by towering oaks.

Voices from the people on the lanai float up on a breeze,
and the music from downstairs *thump-thumps* in the walls
like the house itself has a heartbeat.

"Do you ever dream about flying?" I ask Nalu suddenly.

He considers my question.

"Sometimes. Mostly, though, I dream that I'm back in Hawai'i.
Or that I live underwater." The corners of his mouth twitch.
"Why do you ask?"

"I just think I would be really, really good at it."

I take in a deep breath of cool air, hoping it might do something
to help scrub the drunken fog from my brain.

Nalu chuckles. "How are you doing there?"

I rest my head on his shoulder. "Good . . ."
My voice feels cottony in my mouth. "But maybe too good?"

"How about a cup of water?"

I start to nod but stop quickly when the world starts to spin.
"Ouch.
    Water.
        Yes.
            Please."

"I'll be right back," he assures me.
"Don't go flying off into the night without me, okay?"

I smile after him as he retreats down the hallway. "No promises."

While I wait
for Nalu
to return,
I sway to the songs
of the trees,
listen to their hymns
howled into the night,
look up just in time
to see a crow
twirling down
from the sky,
landing softly
on feathered branches
with its beak open wide
to let out a caw *caw! caw!*
caw!
caw! *caw!*
that sounds more like
a scream *caw!*
caw! than anything
caw!
caw! caw!
caw!
caw!
caw!
caw! caw!
caw!
caw!
caw!

Down the hallway
a door slams shut,
followed
by someone's voice
rising above the party clamor—

I know that voice.

Kāia.

My sister flies
down the hallway, and I swear
for a moment
I see—
no,
I was wrong;
it was just her hair
fluttering like ribbons behind her.

"Kāia?"
When she looks up, my stomach drops
        at the tears in her eyes,
        at the way her chest heaves up and down.
"What happened?"

She brushes me off. "I don't want to talk,
especially not to *you*."

And the way she looks at me feels
like walking away from Nalu that night at the lake,
like Derek's cold lips pressed against mine,
like Taylor trading me in for a new best friend,
like Aunty 'Ehu flying away,
like Gina's name in small, slender handwriting,
like Dad's anger,
like Mama's fear,
like a broken promise,
like falling out of that tree
and hitting the ground,

all over again,
all at once.

"Kāia, what happened?"

"Like you don't know." She laughs, sharp and joyless.

"I really don't."

Her voice drops low. "I *know* what you did."

She looks so much like Dad

when she's angry.

"Kāia—"

"You hooked up with Derek."
She swipes her tears away roughly with the back of her hand.
"At the retreat. Even though you knew how much I liked him—"

My bottom lip starts to tremble.
"Kāia, that's *not* what happened—"

She sniffles. "And tonight,
he—
he—
tried—"

"What did he do?"

I reach for her,
I grab her hand,
I try to keep her here with me—

Kāia freezes.

Suddenly.

Eerily.

"You are . . ." Her voice trembles slightly.

"What, Kāia?"

She snatches back her hand
as if my skin had burned her.

"Nothing." She shakes her head,
as she starts to withdraw

away
away
away from me.

"You are nothing."

I
watch
my sister
leave,
hoping
until

the

very

last

moment

that

she

might

turn

around,

but she never does.

My eyes narrow on the door
my sister ran out of,

and without thinking—or knocking—
I let myself in
to what must be Katie's dad's office.

Everything is made of dark wood.

The floors.
The tall shelves.
The wide desk
where I find Derek Miller,
sitting in a leather chair with his feet up on the edge,
scrolling on his phone like he's bored.

I slam the door shut behind me.
"*What*
did
you
do
to
my
sister?"

I'm flinging,
I'm flying,

my wings are beating
in rhythm with my wild heart.

Derek's eyes flash with annoyance,
then anger,
and then,
he snuffs it all out
before he lets me see too much
                    of who he really is,

a wasteful effort on his part.
I know who he is.
He is the mountain lion,
          and now, I am the deer.

"Nothing." He swings his legs off the desk,
then stands up slowly. "Your prude sister is no fun, but you . . ."
He points a lazy finger in my direction. "You're fun.
She didn't like hearing that, though."

I am scared
when he backs me up against the wall,
when his hand grips my waist,
I
am
terrified
but then I remember—

I

can

fly.

I fly

fly

fly

back into the mess of the party
and end up face-to-face with Taylor.

"Thank God." All I feel is relief,
grabbing on, clinging to her like my life depends on it.
"Have you seen Kāia? I think something bad happened—"

Taylor flicks my fingers from her shoulders.
Her eyes are hazy with alcohol
as she looks me up
and down.

"It's always
something bad,
something *terrible,* with you,
isn't it?"

"Taylor . . ."

She closes her eyes,
presses a hand to her head, waves her cup slowly in the air
as if to ward me off like a fly that won't stop buzzing in her face.

"I'm sick of it, Lily. I'm sick
of you."

By the time I get outside,

Kāia's
car
is
gone.

Nalu finds me sitting alone on the front steps.
"Hey, what did I say about flying away without me?" he teases,
but the grin drops from his face
the moment
he
sees
mine.

"What happened? Are you okay?" He crouches down,
hands hovering over me as he scans my body
for any sign of hurt,

but there is nothing for him
to see;

all my wounds
are on the inside.

Mama and Dad are waiting for me
when I arrive in Nalu's car,   long after
I was supposed to be home,   a little drunk
with my wings stooped low,   and
without
my sister—

but her car is in the driveway.

So I know she is safe.

And for the moment,   that's enough.

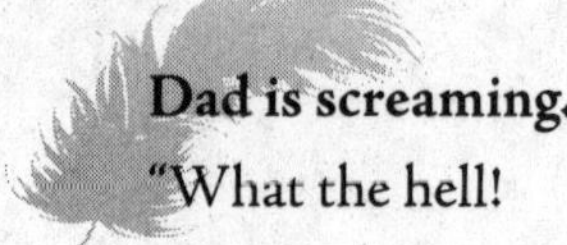

Dad is screaming.

"What the hell!   has gotten!   into you!

And what!

were you doing!   in Nalu's car!"

I struggle
I struggle
I struggle to get the words   out.

"He   drove   me   here."
But it all sounds like a garbled mess to my ears.

Dad slams his fist against the kitchen counter—
my world quakes.

"She's drunk!"

Mama grabs me. "Aouli. Baby."
When was the last time
my mother called me baby?

Surely
sometime
a long time
before
before
before   this great big hole in my chest.

"You're not drunk, right? Right?"

I rip myself out of her cage,
and when I see the hurt in her eyes
it makes me feel good.

Like maybe she will finally feel

a splinter

of the pain

she's caused me.

"I expected more from you,"
Dad says,

and that's the spark
to light the fuse
that
finally
sets
me
off.

"You expected more from me? You expected more from me? You expected more from me? You expected more from me?

What about you, Dad? What about you, Dad? What about you, Dad? What about you, Dad? What about you, Dad?

I expected more from you! I expected more from you! I expected more from you! I expected more from you!

Why must I struggle and struggle to please you? Why must I struggle and struggle to please you? Why must I struggle?

To make you happy? To make you happy? To make you happy? To make you happy? To make you happy?

To be what *you* want me to be? To be what *you* want me to be? To be what *you* want me to be? To be what *you* want me to be?

You have never been what I needed you to be. You have never been what I needed you to be.

I am not tough like you! I am not tough like you! I am not tough like you! I am not tough like you! I am not tough like you!

I am nothing, I am nothing, I am nothing, I am nothing, I am nothing, I am nothing, I am nothing, I am nothing, I am nothing,

I am nothing like you! I am nothing like you! I am nothing like you! I am nothing like you! I am nothing like you!

I expected more! I expected more! I expected more! I expected more! I expected more! I expected more! I expected more!

I deserved more! I deserved more! I deserved more! I deserved more! I deserved more! I deserved more! I deserved more!

You still betrayed us. You still betrayed us. You still betrayed us. You still betrayed us. You still betrayed us. You still betrayed us.

You still betrayed me You still betrayed me You still betrayed me

for—"

Gina Ginha Gina

Gina Gina—

but I can't say it,

even when he waits,

even when I see a hint of understanding in his eyes,

I can't bring my lips to form around this name that

haunts me,

follows me,

holds me down

and cuts   ragged   into my chest.

I look at Mama
and wait

but I've been waiting   for my mother
for a long time   and even when I doubted her
even when I knew she couldn't do it,

I still hoped

that she would one day find the courage
to finally
show up.

I am tired

of waiting.

"I am going to bed," I whisper.
"Take whatever you want from me."

So Dad takes
my wings, locks
my cage, and throws
away the key.

My sister is right,
I am nothing
I am nothing

I am nothing

    I am nothing

I am nothing   I am nothing

I am nothing   I am nothing   I am nothing

    I am nothing   I am nothing I am nothing

I am nothing
I am nothing
I am nothing I am nothing I am nothing I am nothing.

I am nothing **without my wings.**

Part Four

O na hōkū no ka kiu o ka lani.

Hawaiian Proverb

April 5

Easter Sunday of the Resurrection of the Lord

Dear ʻAlalā,
This
would
be
the
perfect
time
for you
to show me
that
you're
listening.

ʻĀmene.

The Punishment

No wings. No wings. No wings. No wings. No wings. No wings.
No wings. No wings. No wings. No wings. No wings. No wings.
No flying.   No freedom.
No flying.   No freedom.
No flying.   No freedom.
No flying.   No freedom.
No flying.   No freedom.
No flying.   No freedom.
No flying.   No freedom.
No flying.   No freedom.
No flying.   No freedom.
No flying.   *Only my cage.*   No freedom.
No flying.   No freedom.
No flying.   No freedom.
No flying.   No freedom.
No flying.   No freedom.
No flying.   No freedom.
No flying.   No freedom.
No flying.   No freedom.
No flying.   No freedom.
No flying.   No freedom.
No flying.   No freedom.
No boys with stars in their eyes. No boys with stars in their eyes.
No boys with stars in their eyes. No boys with stars in their eyes.

After Easter mass,
I sit on the floor of my bedroom
next to the door that I've left open
just   barely
so I can still hear Dad on the phone with Tūtū
as she begs him on my behalf to still let me go
to Hawai'i next week for Aunty 'Ehu's funeral.

After he hangs up the call, I listen intently
to every heavy step he takes
toward me.

"Only because Aunty 'Ehu would have wanted you there," he says,
through the tiny crack of space
before   walking   away.

KOMO 4 EVENING NEWS REPORT
"And now over to Sandra with the weather."

"Thanks, Mark. While the Greater Seattle Area
has enjoyed an unseasonably warm and sunny week,
don't put away those rain jackets just yet!

This evening, expect overcast skies and temperatures to drop
into the midforties. And if we look at the map here,
we can see a stationary front start to form
from Vancouver Island all the way down to Portland.

That means we can all expect
rain,
rain,
and *more* rain,
tomorrow and for the week to come."

April 6

Monday within the Octave of Easter

Mama wakes me up early
to tell me that Dad told her
that Kāia told him
that I will be riding the bus from now on,
because I am no longer welcome in her car.

"So you better get going," Mama whispers.
"And don't forget your rain jacket.
It's really coming down out there."

At lunch,

I pick

at

my food,

but I can't

bring

myself

to

eat.

I toss it all into the trash
on my way out of the lunchroom—

"Lily?"

I freeze, realizing

Taylor,

who hasn't spoken to me
since Saturday night,

followed me into the hallway.

"Can I talk to you? It's important."

I don't answer her;
instead
I turn quickly on my heel
and rush away from her—
        just like she did from me—
as
fast
as
I
can.

I have no idea where Dad stashed my phone
when he took it away Saturday night, so I have
no way to tell Nalu what's happened,
no way to promise him I'm not ignoring him again,
no way to tell him I would fly to him
if only I had my wings.

So after everyone has gone to sleep,
I tiptoe out of my bedroom to search for it—
        but I don't even make it to Dad's office
        before he finds me and escorts me silently
        back to bed.

April 7

Tuesday within the Octave of Easter

Dad talks to me today,
not with his eyes
or from behind a door,
but for real—

but what he doesn't realize is that
I'm not ready yet
to start talking to him.

"Aouli?"

I barely glance up from
my homework.

"Your sister just received
the decision from Yale."

But this makes me look up
all the way.

"Come, she's about to open it
now."

Kāia and Mama are waiting
in Dad's office.

Kāia sits at the computer while
Mama hovers over her.

Dad joins them, taking his place
on Kāia's other side.

I stick to the wall, eager
to make a quick exit as soon

as all the crying and cheering
and *I'm so proud of you*s begin.

"Go ahead." Dad nudges Kāia,
smiling for the first time in two days.

Kāia takes a deep breath,
then clicks the button that will

propel

her

to

her

bright, bright future—

"I didn't get in."

Kāia squeezes her eyes shut
and opens them back up wide,

like maybe
she just isn't seeing straight. "I—"

"Aouli," Dad interrupts her. "Go finish your homework."

My sister's eyes dart across
the room to find mine,
as if to say
don't—
don't leave me.

"Dad—" I start.

He dismisses me
with a quick gesture of his hand. "Go."

Dad
keeps
Kāia and Mama
in his office all night,
in the hopes he might figure out
what he did to deserve
two daughters
who
will
never
be

enough.

April 8

Wednesday within the Octave of Easter

I find Kāia during lunch
in the library, studying.

"Go away," she says,
before I even open my mouth.

"Kāia . . ."

Her fist tightens
around her pencil.

"Get *out.*"

I rush out of the library,
scrubbing my eyes to keep
the tears from falling—

"Lily!"

"Jesus, what do you *want?*"

Taylor stands just outside
the library entrance, and I wonder
if she followed me here.

She holds up a hand. "Please,
don't leave yet. I—I have something
for you."

I cross my arms. "Well. What is it?"

"Oh!" She nods like a bobblehead.
"Yes, it's, uh, right here."

She searches around in her backpack,
then produces a folded piece of paper.
"It's a letter, I think. I didn't read it, I promise."

I eye it suspiciously. "From who?"

"From Nalu."

I take it from her

slowly,

gently,

like it is something precious
and easily breakable.

I hold it to my chest.
"Thank you."

She rocks back and forth
on her feet. "About Saturday—"

But I am already walking away.

Aouli,
Your dad called my dad, and I guess we won't
be able to talk for a while. I'm sorry.

My dad told me to leave you alone, to give you space,
but I didn't want you to think I forgot about you.

I don't think I could if I tried.

I've been listening to your song a lot, and I wonder
if you've had a chance to finish it?

Would you send me the lyrics if you have?
Or send whatever you have?

Or just send something? So I know you got this,
at least.

Just give it to Taylor, she will get it to me.

-Nalu

PS: Don't be too mad at me (or Taylor)
for how I got you this note. I didn't have many options.

Dear ʻAlalā,
Mahalo.
For listening.
For sending me
a shooting star.

ʻĀmene.

Dream
ʻAlalā

visits me

tonight

in my dreams.

She sings

to me

from the bottom of her cage.

"I am always listening,
my daughter."

"Now, please. Let us out."

"We were made to fly."

April 9

Thursday within the Octave of Easter

I'm up early with the rain
pouring outside my window,
pouring my heart
into the pages of my song journal—

and when I finally think I've
got it,

the rain has ebbed and the sun
is breaking through
the clouds.

I tear the pages right out of my notebook,
fold them up tight
and write on the outside:

It's not a song yet
without music.
—Aouli

April 12

Sunday of Divine Mercy

I don't know how she does it,
but Taylor finds a way

to pass notes

back & forth

back & forth

back & forth

back & forth

back & forth

back & forth

between

Nalu & me

every day

until

Sunday.

Dad doesn't allow Kāia and me
to stay after church for youth group,

but on our way out of mass
Taylor manages to slip me a final note from Nalu
when my parents aren't looking.

She presses the neatly folded square of notebook paper
into my palm.

"We figured your dad wouldn't let you stay.
Sorry I can't help during spring break; I'll be at Gram's all week.
It's going to suck."

We share the smallest, briefest smile at that,
and I know we are both remembering the time before
everything
changed.

My fingers curl around the note. "Thanks."

Today his letter is brief—

I'll meet you
on the other side
of the ocean.

-Nalu

April 15

Wednesday

Memory

Eleven Years Ago

Dad is yelling at Mama,
but I don't know what she could have done
that would make his voice
                    rattle the house like thunder.

I am quiet, like a mouse,
when I sneak into my sister's room
and slip beneath the covers.

"Aouli?" Kāia rubs the sleep from her eyes.
"What are you doing?"

"I can't sleep."

Dad's voice rumbles,
          then my sister understands.

Her hand finds mine under the quilt.
I am so little that my fingers barely reach
the tips of hers.

"It's okay," she promises me.
"It will pass."

It's the night before
we fly to Kona, and a spring storm
is raging, wailing
against my
window.

There's a small knock
followed by the *creeeeak* of my door being pushed open.

An eye.
A nostril.
A worried lip.

Kāia lets herself in, shutting the door softly behind her.

"What's wrong?" I ask as she crawls into my bed
and pulls the sheets over her body so only her head pokes out.

She sighs. "Can't sleep."

"The storm?"

"Yeah." She shimmies closer to me,
the warmth of her body pressing against mine.
"Among other things."

Lightning strikes blue,
illuminating my room so I can see

every sharp,
pretty
angle
of my sister's face.

She is beautiful like Mama,
except when she is angry like Dad.

But when she looks at me now,

I only see myself staring back.

I find her hand under the covers.
Force her fingers to twine with mine.
Our hands are the same size now.

A perfect match.

"It's okay," I whisper. "It will pass."

April 16

Thursday

A conversation just before sunrise.

Kāia: I know nothing happened between you and Derek at the retreat.

Me: How . . . ?

Kāia: Nalu.

Kāia: He wrote me a letter.

Me: Damn.

Kāia: What?

Me: I was hoping I was the only girl he was writing letters to.

Kāia: Well, if it helps, his letter to me was *only* about you.

Me: That helps a little.

Kāia: I hate that Derek did that to you. I wish I had known.

Me: There's nothing you could have done.

Kāia: I could have kicked his ass.

Me: I would pay good money to see you try to fight him.

Me: Fight anyone, honestly.

Kāia: Hey, I am in great shape. And stop deflecting, just let me apologize.

Me: Well, by all means.

Kāia: You are impossible.

Kāia: I am sorry for assuming instead of just asking you what happened with Derek and for yelling at you in front of everyone at church and for never backing you up when Dad is coming for you. I've been—

Me: Scared?

Kāia: Terrified.

Me: I am sorry, too.

Kāia: Why are you sorry?

Me: For a little bit of everything.

Kāia: Well, I forgive you.

Me: I forgive you, too.

"We are leaving for the airport in an hour!"
Dad yells from the kitchen, as someone knocks on my door.

"Come in!"

I'm standing over my empty suitcase
and a pile of clean laundry
that was supposed to be packed last night.

Kāia enters but stops short at the sight of my mess.
"Aouli, you were supposed to be packed last—"

I wave her off. "Last night, yeah, yeah."

"You need to work on your time management skills,"
she remarks as she sits down on the floor
crisscross beside my pile.

My eyebrow perks. "What are you doing?"

She doesn't look at me—

she just starts folding.

"Helping you."

A conversation as we pack.

Kāia: Nalu is a good writer.

Me: I know.

Kāia: Smart, too.

Me: You're telling me.

Kāia: Super hot.

Me: Hey!

Kāia: What? I'm just saying . . .

Me: Well, *just say it* in your head.

Kāia: How do I get a smart *and* hot guy?

Kāia: I can't even get a guy with one of those attributes.

Me: You got to pray on it.

Kāia: Aouli.

Me: What? That's what I did.

Kāia: You have got to be kidding me.

After our plane lands at the Kona airport,
all four of us walk out to find Tūtū waiting for us
curbside in Papa's old truck.
We have to squish in to fit,
but we make it work
and soon we're on a road heading north that winds
this way   and that,
cutting
through
black rock that runs   far and   wide.

I press my cheek up against the window
to watch the land lurch and fall away,
to see the tall grass that sprouts between the ʻaʻā,
    a reminder that life
    is always springing up
    in the most unlikely of places.

April 17

Friday

Being back in Tūtū's yard,
with my limbs splayed long in the grass,
it's all too easy to lose myself in the vast blue sky above.

"Aouli?" Kāia surprises me,
her steps softer than the ocean's breeze.
    She's still in her pajamas, a sunshine-yellow set.

"Hey." I sit up slowly, curling my knees into my chest as she drops to sit beside me. "What's up?"

She fiddles with the edge of her sleeve, straightening a wrinkle in the fabric. "I thought maybe I could do your hair for today?"

"You want to do my *hair*?"

> Of all the things I could have guessed
> that my sister came out to say to me,
>
> asking to do my hair was the absolute last.

Kāia sits up a little straighter, leaving her sleeve alone. "And your makeup, too."

"Kāia. It's Aunty's funeral." I lie back down in the grass, folding my hands over my stomach. "Not prom."

She considers me for a moment before lying down
next to me,
shoulder to shoulder,
hip to hip.

"I know. I just thought it might be nice—"

but then I start laughing,
and I don't know how
to
stop.

At first Kāia is confused,
and then she's laughing, too,
and I'm grabbing her arm to keep myself steady,
and she's tugging on my shoulder to anchor
herself down,
and we're laughing so hard tears stream down both our faces,
so hard my stomach starts to ache,
so hard that I have no choice but to keep laughing
until I can be sure
I've shaken all the laughter out—

we are not soft or gentle or quiet,

but wild and untamed,
rolling around out here in the grass.

My sister sighs
as her laughter
dies
out.
She watches me
with careful eyes and brushes away a

stray tear

from my face.

I let Kāia do my hair
        and my makeup, too.

"This is like real sister shit," I say,
watching her in the mirror
as she wraps a section of my hair
around the hot barrel of her curling iron.

She chuckles. "We are real sisters."

Yeah.
                                We are.

When we arrive at the church
for the funeral, I waste no time
looking for Nalu
amid the swelling sea
of friends
and family arriving
                        from near
                                and far—

but despite my best efforts,
I come up short.

"He's not here," I whisper to Kāia.

She squeezes my hand.
"He will be."

The church beside the sea
fills quickly to the edges with everyone
here to say their goodbyes
to Aunty ʻEhu,

but it feels wrong
to let this be her last moment,
to let the last thing she sees be this ceiling,

this cage.

Dad finds me against the wall,
avoiding
avoiding
avoiding
avoiding
saying goodbye.

He nudges me forward.

"Go."

I place
my hand flat
against the smooth surface
of the urn,

fingers brushing
the delicate white and yellow petals
of plumeria strung together to adorn
the polished vessel.

"A hui hou, Aunty.
I'll see you in my dreams."

And,
I
know,

I know I will.

Dear ʻAlalā,

Watch

over

my aunty

as

she

finds

her

way

back

to

the

sky.

ʻĀmene.

Dad and Mama
busy themselves after the service,
making sure to talk to everyone,
        while my sister and I try our best
        to just stay out of the way.

"Hey." Kāia bumps my shoulder with hers.
"Look who it is."

My heartbeat picks up;
he must have gotten here
after the funeral had already started
and I was no longer paying attention to the entrance.

But there he is now,

        a boy with stars in his eyes,

waiting for me   across   the room.

Nalu stands with Keala
while their dad chats in a small group of adults.

I wait until he looks,
then I tilt my head toward the exit.

He smiles, nodding his chin ever so slightly,
before leaning down to whisper something to his sister.

And once I'm sure Mama and Dad aren't paying attention,
    I slip out a side door,
    knowing Nalu won't be far behind.

I wait for him beside a wall of lava rock
    stacked together like a puzzle
    and hot to the touch under the Kona sun.

"Aouli."

Nalu greets me with the same grin
I've been dreaming of all week long.

I want to throw my arms around him,
hug him,
kiss him,
tell him—

But he holds up his ukulele. "I have something for you.
Quick, before they notice we're gone."

Nalu leads
me
across
the road
and down
a sandy
path
between
the rocks
where
we're
greeted
first
by
the
whisper
of the
ocean,
and
then
the
rush
of the
wind
as the
beach
opens up
before us
and my world is engulfed by

the big blue sky big blue sky big blue sky big blue sky big blue sky big blue sky big blue sky big blue sky big bluc sky big blue sky **and the big blue sea** big blue sea.

This is where
he begins to play
a song,

my song.

"You did that for me?"
I whisper when he's done.

He shrugs.

"You said it wasn't a real song
until it had music."

And like the big blue sky
                and the big blue sea,

my words
        and his music   together
        make something whole and complete.

This is where I tell him,
here with my eye on the horizon
to keep me brave,
about
Taylor
Kāia
Mama
Dad
Gina—

This is where I tell him everything.

When I'm done
we are both silent for a long while.
But it doesn't feel bad;

it feels like the space
I needed
to finally start to heal.

We stay here a little longer than we should,
sitting just close enough to the edge
of the water so the foamy surf rolls
over our toes as the tide goes
in
and out.

At some point Nalu reaches for me,
and curling into him feels like coming home.

And when I look at him
I
finally
get
it,

that the ocean is just a reflection
of what the sky can never see,
that the stars that shine so brightly
in his eyes have always been a reflection
of
the
skies
inside
of
me.

Before people start to arrive at Tūtū's house tonight,
I help set up the backyard with Kāia and our cousin.

We cover long folding tables in pink paper tablecloths—
Aunty ʻEhu's favorite color—
while my uncle works on hanging rows of yellow string lights
so that the celebration for the woman
who always loved a good party
can go well into the night.

As we finish,
I stand back to look at our work. "What do you think, Nohealani?"

My cousin catches my hand in hers
as she throws her other arm around my sister's shoulders,
pullingusinclose—
just like how Aunty ʻEhu used to.

"She would have loved this."

Hundreds of people show up
to celebrate Aunty ʻEhu's life,
and I see her
e v e r y w h e r e,

in the music
in the dancing
in the prayer
in the food
in the gossip
in the laughter
in the tears
in my cousins
in my uncles
in my aunties
in Nalu
in Keala
in their father
in Tūtū
in Mama
in Dad
in Kāia
in the last flare of sunlight
          in the stars just come out to shine
                    in a night that's perfect for flying

in myself   every time   I catch a glimpse
of her in my reflection—
in the proud tilt of my chin, in the set of my shoulders,
in the determination flashing in my eyes—

I see her, like she's right here with me. Like she never left.

Nalu and I
watch each other
move through the night.
Eyes always searching for the other,
fingers brushing,
touching when they can,
our hearts always finding their way back
even after being
swept away
in the break.

When I find him again,
I lift my mouth to his ear,

then
I
let
him
lead
me
away.

Nalu takes me six houses down the street
to his grandmother's, leading me
through the garage
where her dog is wagging his tail
like he's been waiting for us all night.

I rub his big belly when he rolls over.
"I remember you from the pictures."

"Hey, Pepe, boy." Nalu scratches Pepe's chin,
and I laugh, watching his tail wag so hard
it beats against his sides—

Nalu looks back at me over his shoulder
with an expression I can't quite name.

"Is something wrong?"

"No, nothing is wrong." He turns back to Pepe.
"I just like your laugh."

Nalu's room is small.
A bed.
A nightstand.
A lamp.
Pictures of him and Keala through the years,
surf posters, and skate stickers decorate the walls.

He stuffs his hands deep into his pockets.
"No one will be home for a while."

I swallow and try not to let my nerves
get the best of me,

because I am not what was expected,

I am not soft,
gentle,
or quiet.

I am so much more.

We come

together,

melding into
one,

like that place

where the sky
meets the sea.

I rest my head on Nalu's chest
and listen to the beat of his heart.

Thump-thump, thump-thump, thump-thump.

Music.

"Hey!" I blink once, twice, three times,
not believing what I see
when I glance
up.

"I used to have those on my ceiling, too."
I point at the glow-in-the-dark stars.

"Yeah?" His fingers trail down the back of my arm.
"My tūtū tried to take them down once, and I cried," he admits.
"But I was like ten."

I laugh. "Really?"

"Really." He sighs.
"I think a part of me has always loved the sky."

April 18

Saturday

Today is our last full day in Kona
before we have to go back home tomorrow,

and Dad is angry this morning
because Mama didn't load the dishwasher right last night,
because Kāia refused to email Yale Admissions
about why she was rejected,
because I disappeared from the party and didn't tell him
where I was going,

because we have never been good enough
for him.

We do our best to dodge his rage.

Tūtū tucks herself away in her bedroom,

Mama fusses over the dishes,

trying to fix her mistake, I keep

my head down at the dining table,

resigned to stay out of the way

as Kāia pads quietly into the kitchen,

quiet as she's ever been, reaching

into the cabinet for a mug,

doing her best

to keep herself

small, but

Dad just

won't

stop.

"Dad, ***please,"***
Kāia pleads, as he digs harder into Mama.
"Please, stop."
But he   is not   listening.
"Dad."
Kāia tries again,
but
still
she
is
ignored.

And I watch the rage start to gather
like storm clouds
across my sister's face
the moment she decides she will no longer
keep herself   small—

and
she
slams
the
mug
down—
crack!—
sending
hundreds

of

tiny

pieces

scattering

across
the

tile.

Kāia drops to the floor,
and her apologies sing
like the refrain of a heartbreak song.

"I'm sorry.
I'm sorry.
I'm sorry.
I'm sorry."

Dad flushes red,
eyes darkening,
fists clenching.

Mama steps back, casting her gaze downward
as if not seeing
could absolve her—

Dad's words fly.

"Lazy!"

"Careless!"

"Not thinking!"

"Never thinking!"

"Never!"

Each syllable striking my sister, drawing blood, leaving
scars. And Mama does nothing.

I am tired

of nothing,
of waiting for her
to show up.

She's never going to show up.

My wings
unfurl,
crashing,
slapping,
filling up the space.
My body flies
to cover my sister,
to take each accusation,
every ugly word he slings,
to shield her with my wings
from that which has cut
us both

so

deep.

Dad
never
took my wings.

They were always mine.

And for the first time ever,
Dad sees all of me.

Kāia looks up, resolve
hardening her gaze, and then I see
what I thought I saw that night at the party,

and I know she's always had wings, too.

We stand together
in front of our mother,
because I don't know
if she has wings,

but her daughters do.

"Stop, Dad." Kāia's voice is strong and steady.

I hold my chin high, nodding. "You have said enough."

Dad is silent
for the rest of the day,
and even if it is just for this brief moment,
there
is
finally
peace.

Dream
Aunty ʻEhu
strokes
the silky black
feathers of ʻAlalā.

And when I look in her eyes, I see my own.

Bright. Green. Alert.

And full of life.

April 19

Third Sunday of Easter

Dad is up before everyone else.
I find him alone

in the backyard,
watching the sky,

and I wonder what he's looking for

and if he will ever find it.

Can I ask you something?"
I startle him.

He frowns, turning his back to me
again. "Sure."

"I keep having these dreams . . ."

I expect him to
brush me off,
to scold me,
to punish me for suggesting
that maybe,
just maybe
I was visited by a spirit,
a phantom,
a ghost?
But instead, he is quiet as he listens
to me recount my dreams.

"'Uhane," he says, when I'm done. "It is called 'uhane."

I search his face
for disappointment,
for resentment,
for anger,

but for a second,
there is only a jolt of light
in his green eyes,
which are green like my eyes.

Alert and full of life, too.

He nods, solemn. "I've had those dreams, too."

And though the road will be a long and weary one ahead,
I think I just stumbled upon a new path.

I just don't know
if I am ready
to take it.

'Uhane.
A soul.
A spirit.
A memory.

The thing that remains.

What we are
once what was made
can no longer carry

our magic.

Kāia and I go to the beach,
just the two of us,
one last time before our flight.

"I have to tell you something."

"Is it bad?" she asks.

And finally, I trust my sister
with the truth. "Yeah, it's bad."

She sighs, reaching out to grab my hand,

and her touch
is the last bit of spackle
to fill up the hole in my chest.

Bright

red

sun—

with hands on either side of me,
my sister pulls me up to take the cross
off my back and lay it

across her own.

April 20

Monday

Kāia takes us on a detour on the way to school
so we can get lattes and drink them in the car together,
even though she knows it will make us both late for class.
All the things I never thought my sister and I would do.

"What now?" she asks.
"If Mama doesn't want to do anything about it?"

I thumb the lip of the flimsy plastic coffee lid. "I don't know."

She sighs. "Me neither."

I smile.

Her face falls. "What?"

"Nothing. It's just refreshing to hear you admit
you don't have all the answers
all the time."

She clicks her tongue, sipping her latte to hide her own smile
budding on her face.

We walk to class together through the emptying halls
as a warning bell goes off.

"It's official," Kāia says. "I accepted the offer
from the University of Washington this morning."

"How do you feel?"

"Good," she says, though I don't find her answer
to be very believable. "It will be fine," she reassures me,
even though it sounds more like
she's trying to reassure herself.

"Hey, at least I'll be close. I can come up and visit you—"
I gasp, grabbing her hand. "You can take me to a party!"

She laughs. "Absolutely not."

When the last bell of the day rings,
Taylor is waiting for me outside my sixth-period class.

"I haven't been a good friend," she says, the words rushing out
of her mouth.

"Yes." I nod. "True."

She deflates a bit, and I can't believe she really thought
I would forgive her just like that.

"Think we could ever go back?" she asks, her voice quiet.
"You know, to how we were before?"

And I want to say yes—

but then I feel my wings flutter to life, reminding me
of everything that's changed.

"I don't think so."

Kāia's waiting at the end of the hallway,
watching Taylor walk away over my shoulder.
"You okay?"

"Yeah." And I really, actually am.

We walk together to the parking lot
while she tells me
about French class
and drill team drama
and her lazy lab partner
who never does his homework
and everything else
she never could
tell me
before,

and it takes everything in me
not to throw my arms around her and squeal.

This is my sister!
This is my sister!
This is my sister!
This is my sister!
This is my sister!
This is my sister!
This is my sister!
This is *my* sister!

Kāia spots Nalu first,
but it doesn't take long for my eyes
to find his.

They will always find him.

He's waiting for me next to his truck,
with a big grin on his face.

My heartbeat quickens,
and my wings start to beat,

reminding me that

I am not broken.
I am here.
I am alive.
I am whole.
I am brave.
I am tough like my father.
I am wild like my aunty.
I am every star in the sky.
I am the ocean that loves me.
I am made for soaring

like my sister,
like ʻAlalā,
like my ancestors before me.

Kāia whispers. "Go already."

We meet

and my wings

spread

wide
w i d e
w   i   d   e

his heart
mine too

fly

fly

fly

to that place

where the sky
meets the sea.

ʻŌLELO HAWAIʻI GLOSSARY

ʻaʻā (ah-AH): Rough lava rock.

ʻae (aye): Yes.

A hui hou (ah-hoo-ee-ho): Until I see you again.

ʻAlalā (ah-la-LA): Crow; a loud trill.

ʻĀmene (AH-meh-neh): Amen.

ʻaumakua (ah-ma-coo-ah): Family god; deified ancestor.

ʻEhu (eh-hoo): Red hair (specifically Polynesians with red hair).

heʻe (hey-eh): Octopus.

hele (he-lay): Go.

ʻiʻi (ee-ee): A guttural tremor used in singing and chanting.

i ka wā kahiko (ee-cah-VA-kah-hee-ko): In the old time; in the old days.

ipu (ee-poo): Musical instrument made from a gourd.

keiki (kay-kee): Children.

lauhala (la-ow-ha-la): Leaves of the hala tree, often dried and then used to weave.

mahalo (ma-ha-low): Thank you.

Mahina (ma-hee-nah): Full moon.

Mauna Loa (ma-ow-nah-low-ah): Active volcano on the island of Hawaiʻi.

moʻo (mo-oh): Gecko.

muʻumuʻu (moo-oo-moo-oo): A loose dress.

nānū (nah-noo): Gardenia.

ʻŌlelo Hawaiʻi (OH-lell-oh-ha-vai-ee): Hawaiian language.

O na hōkū no ka kiu o ka lani (oh-nah-ho-coo-no-kah-kee-oo-oh-ka-la-nee): The stars are the spies of the sky (meaning the stars look down on everyone and everything).

pāhoehoe (pah-hoi-hoi): Smooth lava rock.

pīkake (pee-kah-kay): Jasmine.

pōhaku (PO-ha-coo): Rock, stone, or pebble (but in this novel it is referring to a pōhaku ku'i 'ai, which is a stone tool used to pound poi).

pua manu (poo-ah-mah-noo): Bird-of-paradise flower.

pule (poo-lay): Prayer.

wai (ve-ay): Fresh water.

NAMES AND THEIR MEANINGS

Aouli (ah-oo-lee): Sky; blue vault of heaven.

Kāia (ka-AY-ah): Fast asleep.

Kōnane (KO-nah-nay): Bright moonlight.

Nalu (na-loo): Waves; surf; ocean.

JAPANESE GLOSSARY

Bachan (BATCH-an): Grandmother

PIDGIN (HAWAIIAN CREOLE ENGLISH) GLOSSARY

maddah: Mother.

faddah: Father.

ho: Hey!

fo': For.

Local music: Refers to contemporary Hawaiian music.

kine: Kind.

old fut: Old fart (old person).

slippahs: Flip-flops.

whatevah: Whatever.

A NOTE FROM THE AUTHOR

Aloha nō, Reader,

In my hands you hold my heart. Thank you for being so gentle with it.

This story was born out of something very real that happened to me. Not long after my grandfather passed away in 2019, my Aunty Marie, his sister, passed as well. That night, she visited me in a dream and told me she was there to let me know that my grandfather was okay. That is why this book is, in part, dedicated to Aunty Marie—for not only bringing me peace in letting me know my papa's soul was safe but for showing me that my ancestors are always watching over me.

This book is many things. A love story—in every sense. A protest. A prayer. An exploration of grief and the beauty that often arises out of those tough moments. Ultimately, however, it is a question of faith: Who deserves our devotion and why?

Growing up, I always wished I believed in God the way my family did. I yearned for that sort of devout faith, to feel like I had all the answers and everything figured out. I wanted to believe in something bigger than myself and to not feel so alone in this strange world of ours. I wanted a guarantee that everything would work out. At the end of the book, Aouli doesn't have the guarantees she wanted. She doesn't know why her mother can't find the strength to protect her or why her father cheated, or even if the affair will ever end. She doesn't know what the future holds for her family, and that is *frustrating*; I get it.

But, Reader, she knows this:

That love is real. That all wounds heal. That music is everywhere. That new paths can always be forged, and that you have the choice whether to take them or not. That our ancestors are always there to help us—you just have to ask. That the stars will continue to shine to light the way home. And finally, that no creature made for soaring can ever truly be contained by a cage.

Me ka ha'aha'a,
Kauakanilehua

A NOTE FROM CYNTHIA LEITICH SMITH, AUTHOR-CURATOR OF HEARTDRUM

Dear Reader,

Aouli's story blooms from love—romantic love, sisterly love, love put to the test, and love for an ocean-kissed place that will always be home, no matter how far away she may be or for how long. That doesn't mean Aouli's life is all gentle tides and soft moonlight. In trying to put a bow on girlhood, too often this uncertain world can make us feel like we're tied in knots.

I bet you know what that's like.

Love brings challenges, but it's the answer, too. Be sure to love yourself. You deserve it.

You deserve it. You deserve it. You deserve it. You deserve all the love in the world.

Have you read many stories by and about Native Hawaiians or other Indigenous people? Hopefully, *An Expanse of Blue* will inspire you to read more. The novel is published by Heartdrum, an imprint of HarperCollins that focuses on books about young Native heroes by Indigenous authors and illustrators.

I'm delighted that we've published author Kauakanilehua Māhoe Adams's first novel. She writes with thoughtful tenderness about the clear blue skies and waves of gray in families, friendships, and first everythings with a special someone.

This story is called "a novel in verse." In the white spaces between the words, maybe you caught reflections of your own life. If you're struggling—or soaring—like Aouli, consider putting your thoughts into poetic form. It can be healing, celebratory, even cathartic. If not all the words come right away, that's okay. Make space for them. Make space for your feelings, even if you don't yet fully understand them. Make space for yourself. Again, you deserve it.

Mvto,
Cynthia Leitich Smith

ACKNOWLEDGMENTS

Mahalo nui to everyone who made my debut novel a reality (there are a lot of you).

Rosemary Brosnan, my editor, you are a superstar. Thank you for not only challenging me to stretch myself as a poet and a storyteller but for loving this story as much as I do. You made a little Hapa girl's far-fetched dream a reality the day you called me to tell me you wanted to publish this book. Thank you (from both of us). Cynthia Leitich Smith, author-curator, storyteller, teacher, mentor, friend, you are all of the above and more. You saw something in this story when I didn't, and I am forever (and ever and ever and ever) grateful. Sara Crowe, my dream agent! Thank you for so fearlessly guiding me through every twist, turn, and long wait that comes with publishing a book.

Thank you to Melanie Crowder, who read the first wobbly-legged draft of this book, for encouraging me to write Aouli's story in verse. Mahalo nui from the bottom of my heart for reminding me *I am* a poet. To Christine Hartman-Derr, soul sister, confidante, and best roommate ever, I am so grateful we get to go on this crazy journey of publishing together. Ty Chapman, brilliant storyteller but most importantly, my cherished friend, thank you for sitting on Google Meet with me for hours during those months that I wrote this story. Your companionship and steadfast encouragement kept me writing forward. Caroline

Cullinane, Mckenna Rice, Alexis Powell, Mary Neville, and Ty (again!)—I won the friendship jackpot with all of you. Thank you for being my number one fans since day one. You each are as magnificent as the full moon on a clear night—big, bright, and worthy of marveling! Thank you to my best friend, Madison Stuart, for reading this book in a day. We may never know what you said about it in that long-lost eight-minute voice note, but I bet it was both thought-provoking and wise—as everything you say often is. I can't wait to be old ladies together. Mahalo nui to Keala Kendall, Kealani Netane, and Malia Maunakea for reading the first real draft of Aouli's story. You are the Kānaka Maoli authors of my dreams, the ones whose stories I longed for as a child and get to read as an adult today. Thank you to my ever-growing Native writing community: my fellow Heartdrum authors; all the participants, staff, and faculty of the We Need Diverse Books Native Writing Intensives; all the Pacific Islanders in Publishing; and especially Cynthia Leitich Smith, Christine Hartman-Derr, Keliko Adams, Karina Iceberg, Stacy Wells, Leslie Wiedner, AJ Eversole, and Keala Kendall—you are my home.

Thank you to my family, my friends, and my community for keeping me afloat as I've navigated this new and unfamiliar path. To my brother, Ka'ohuokalanipō, and my sister, Anuhea, you are my everything. To my sisters-in-law, Claire and Alycia, and my brothers-in-law, Mason and Blad, I adore each of you to the stars and back. To my dear nephew, Julian, your joy and curiosity for the world we live in is a gift. I will do everything in my power to ensure you grow up in a world with stories about us and our people. Mahalo to my cousin Aja for being the official unofficial Pidgin Consultant for this novel. Womb to the tomb, baby! I love you forever and ever. To my father, for sharing his love of Hawaiian music with me. And to my mother, who stapled together construction paper so I could write my first book of poetry, thank you for sharing the magic of stories with me. To the best friends in the whole dang world—Jacey, Ashton, Henley, Gabby, Jessica, Caroline, Mary, Madison—thank you for loving me through every phase and for standing beside me on my wedding day. And a special thanks to Jace, Ash, and Hen; we've been best friends for so long, there isn't a word great enough to describe how important you three are to me. Thank you for showing me that true love is real.

To Charlie, the love of my life. Thank you for every cup of coffee, clean load of laundry, empty kitchen sink, sweet treat, big hug, and encouraging word. And thank you for hyping me and this book up to anyone who will listen with a kid-in-a-candy-store level of enthusiasm—it's embarrassing, but gosh do I really appreciate it. Thank you for keeping me grounded, for reminding me that I am real, for loving me and all my rough and poky edges. What a ride this has been! I am so glad you are taking it with me.

Mahalo nui to my ancestors for watching over me, for protecting me, for guiding me. To Tūtū and Grandma and Grandpa, I only am because of you. And to my papa, I miss you, I miss you, I miss you.

And finally to all nā keiki Kānaka Maoli on the islands and across the sea, no matter where you are or what you look like, you are Hawaiian enough. *You* are enough.

KAUAKANILEHUA MĀHOE ADAMS

is a mixed Kānaka Maoli (Native Hawaiian) author and poet born and raised in Washington State. She earned her master of fine arts in Writing for Children and Young Adults from Vermont College of Fine Arts. *An Expanse of Blue* is her debut verse novel for young adults.

Kaua lives in Carlsbad, California, with her husband, where she spends her time writing, reading, daydreaming, dancing hula, and bending to her dogs' every wish and whim.

CYNTHIA LEITICH SMITH

is a bestselling, acclaimed author of books for all ages, including *Here Come the Aunties!*, *Firefly Season*, *Jingle Dancer*, *Indian Shoes*, *On a Wing and a Tear*, *Sisters of the Neversea*, *Blue Stars: Mission One: The Vice Principal Problem* (with Kekla Magoon), *Rain Is Not My Indian Name*, *Harvest House*, and *Hearts Unbroken*, which won the American Indian Youth Literature Award. Cynthia is also the anthologist of *Ancestor Approved: Intertribal Stories for Kids* and *Legendary Frybread Drive-In: Intertribal Stories*. She has been honored with the American Library Association's Children's Literature Lecture Award and has been named the NSK Neustadt Laureate. She is the author-curator of Heartdrum, a Native-focused imprint at HarperCollins Children's Books, and served as the Katherine Paterson Endowed Chair on the faculty of the MFA program in Writing for Children and Young Adults at Vermont College of Fine Arts. Cynthia is a citizen of the Muscogee Nation and lives in Denton, Texas.

In 2014, We Need Diverse Books (WNDB) began as a simple hashtag on Twitter. The social media campaign soon grew into a 501(c)(3) nonprofit with a team that spans the globe. WNDB is supported by a network of writers, illustrators, agents, editors, teachers, librarians, and book lovers, all united under the same goal—to create a world where every child can see themselves in the pages of a book. You can learn more about WNDB programs at diversebooks.org.